Aroma

By

Jim Connolly

Other books by same author
Billy's Day (novel)
The Long And Short of It (short stories)
Writing as Jimmy White

This book is copyrighted no part of it can be copied in any form.

This is a work of fiction. Names, characters, businesses, places, events and incidents are either the products of the author's imagination or used in a fictitious manner. Any resemblance to actual persons, living or dead, or actual events is purely coincidental.

ISBN-13: 978-1548025526
ISBN-10: 1548025526

Aroma

3	Chapter 1
16	Chapter 2
29	Chapter 3
42	Chapter 4
63	Chapter 5
72	Chapter 6
83	Chapter 7
101	Chapter 8
112	Chapter 9
121	Chapter 10
131	Chapter 11
149	Chapter 12
167	Chapter 13
182	Chapter 14
196	Chapter 15
214	Chapter 16
227	Chapter 17
250	Chapter 18
270	Chapter 19

Chapter 1

Tethered camels stirred and began an abrasive coughing that shattered the stillness of the desert.

Horses started an answering chorus of whinnies and snorts. A voice shouted in Arabic, questioning, guttural curses echoed on the warm air as a man darted to the shelter of one of the tents that made a multicoloured splash in the moonlight.

"Balek"

The word hung in the scent-laden ambience then, the exhortation to "take care" was repeated sibilant whisperings making a background to the footsteps rustling in the dry grass, loud, fading, voices dying away, the animals quieting....

Ben Acate, heart pounding, eased warily from his place of concealment and made his way to the most ornate of flimsy structures that surrounded him.

Abu Kohani, a large oasis that was once one of the main stopping places for the great caravans that traversed the vast deserts, and long since ignored as more modern forms of transport took a different route to the cities, throbbed with activity as the Kohani Bedouin gathered for their annual festival...

The mating of the racing camels!

The reputation of the Kohani camel-breeders was legendary, and the coming together at this traditional site served to enhance this reputation, for this is where the finest of breeds would be mated, and afterwards taken to the many different 'Souks' the markets of the desert.

For days now, groups of Kohani had travelled from the farthest reaches of the sandy wastes, each set of arrivals being the cause of much feasting and dancing, the greeting of old friends and the settling of outstanding scores. The men if tribes congregated to drink gallons of over-sweet coffee while the women, traditionally, busied themselves with the more mundane tasks of the massive camp-site.

On the morrow the mating would take place.

Racing camels, the haughty Dromedaries, would be bought and sold, females bringing a higher price if they were young and, no less a personage than the Sheikh of Sheikhs, the said, would, with his own hands, apply the special potion to any animals that failed, or were in any way loath, to perform according to their master's wishes.

The potion, a secret formula that Kohani lore maintained had been handed down through the ages by the father of all true Bedouin, the prophet Ishmael, was in the personal safe-keeping of the 'Said' himself and was only taken and used at this time, the time of the mating.

So it was that the night passed. It's tenuous wings unfolding to admit the sneaking rays of the morning sun. then the swiftly rising orb threw bare the shadows and laid open to the rape of the desert heat, the camp, and those, who even now were answering the call of the Muezzin to face Mecca and thank the one true god for delivering them through the passage of darkness. The Sheikh of Sheikhs was breakfasting in his tent when,

"Salaam Aleichum", the greeting was accompanied by a sweeping bow, and the 'Said' nodded his head in return.

"Aleichum us Salaam", the chief smiled, for what father would not smile at the sight of his eldest son standing tall, straight, respectful.

"You gladden an old man's eyes Tariq, sit" he patted the cushions where he himself reclined as he picked up a heaped platter fruit, dates, and the sweetmeats of which he was particularly fond. His son refused the invitation.

"The time is almost upon us father"

The Said inclined his head gravely,

"Aye my son, and as the prophet wills, so shall it be".

He took from his robe a key,

"You shall bring me the potion, for it may not be too long before you will have it's secret and the burden of it's safety for your own

"Many moons will pass and you my father will still be counting them"

The Said smiled.

"Go my silver tongued offspring, go, before you bring my demise with the weight of your

flattery, Allah rules and specifies one's time and I, his humble servant bow to Kismet."
Tariq took the proffered key and stepped to the entrance of his father's sleeping quarters. He bent to an ornate chest that stood just inside, then,
"Father, it's open", bewilderment giving way to panic as he turned, "It's gone, the potion has gone!"
The Said rolled from his cushions and stood, "Guards!" he called, "Bring the guards".
He strode to the chest and saw that the potion was indeed gone, then taking Tariq by the arm, said,
"Come my son, we will achieve nothing here".
The sun was almost vertical in the sky before the Said, after listening to the men who had gathered in front of his tent, discovered that there had been a disturbance during the previous night. Excited voices babbled on accusingly, then defensively, suddenly a name was mentioned, that of Ben Acate. The Sheikh of Sheikhs held up an imperious hand, silence fell,
"Ben Acate?" the Said stroked his chin

thoughtfully.

"Was he here? Surely, did he not go to the city?"

A hubbub of sound rose again and the chief glared as he shouted at them to cease.

"You", he pointed a finger at the one of the men, "You interrupted me, thoughtlessly. Does your chief have no right for his own voice to be heard?"

Crestfallen, the hapless Berber shuffled his feet, his eyes downcast.

"Speak!" ordered the Sheikh,

"And beseech Allah for forgiveness if your words are not worthy of my ears".

"I saw him exalted one. I thought it was strange that he should be here, returned from his adopted country".

The sheikh raised an enquiring eyebrow,

"England" the Arab said, "Ben Acate travelled to England" he made obeisance and shuffled back into the press of onlookers.

"So", intoned the Chief

"This is true?"

A chorus of assent answered his question.

"Mmm", the Said beckoned to Tariq and led

him into his tent
"You heard?"
"Yes my father".
"Then to England he must return, and you, you must follow him, catch him before he leaves our shores, but, if you must, go all the way to this England, bring back the potion, save the face of your father, and the honour of your family."
"Your wish is my command father", Tariq embraced his parent, "And what of Ben Acate?" he asked
"Must he be brought back to be punished"?
The Sheikh stared hard at Tariq.
"Punished", their eyes locked, then as the old man made a slicing motion across his throat with the edge of his hand, the son nodded knowingly,
"It shall be done father".

"I beg your pardon"?
Oliver Trent almost shouted the question at the swarthy faced man who had spoken.
The Birmingham Exhibition Centre throbbed

with the noise of many hundreds of people who thronged the great hall and milled about the dozens of trade stands of which his was one. Again he asked,

"What was it you said?"

The man raised his voice

"You buy?"

Oliver shook his head,

"Did you say buy?" then when the man nodded,

"Look come behind the stand", he led the way.

"This is our hospitality room, it's quieter here. Sit down, drink?" he took an already filled glass from a tray, then, when it was refused, "Oh well, shame to waste it", he sipped, then sat facing the man.

"Now, what's this about, are you an exhibitor?" The Arab stared blankly and Oliver laughed. "Sorry, it means you show things, but what is it you're flogging?"

"Flogging"? The visitor sounded mystified,

"No, no, er this flogging, I have, well" he struggled with his words.

"My name is Ben Acate, I am an Arab, a Kohani, and I now stay in Bradford which is seventy kilometres, er miles from here, I believe I..."

"Yes" Oliver interrupted, "I have a pretty good idea where Bradford is, but, what are you doing here? And what is it you're selling?"

"My apologies", said Ben Acate,"I thought as this is a market-place I could sell here".

"No" said Oliver, shaking his head gravely, "You've got it wrong. This is a trade show, you know, we show our goods, take orders and ..." he paused as a thought struck him.

"Mind you, perhaps you are right, it is a market really, in effect it is anyway, what have you got?"

"Ah", Ben Acate leaned back in his seat, "I do not carry it with me, but it is a potion, it is used at the mating of the camels by the Chief of the Kohani, it aids, er, the ..."

"Sorry my friend" Oliver stopped him; "We don't have camels in this country".

"You do not understand" Ben Acate sat forward, "All animals, horses, any animal, it encourages them".

Oliver smirked as he stood and helped himself to another drink.

"No good for me then, I don't need any encouragement".

He resumed his seat.

"Interesting though, how much do you produce? Is it made here, can you?"

He stopped then,

"There I go, not letting you get a word in, but what quantity are we talking about, hoe many gallons?"

Ben Acate studied him.

"What is gallons? I have this much,"

He held up his thumb and his forefinger spanning three or four inches.

Oliver grinned.

"Not a shipping order, I mean, you've got a sample eh?"

Ben Acate nodded as Oliver continued,

"Not a lot of good to anyone, least of all me, you see, we make plastic mouldings," he sipped his drink, "Hang on though, I know a chap who may be interested. He's with a firm I used to work for". He stood up.

"You wait here, have a drink, eat some of those nuts, shan't be long". He walked from the stand and threaded his way through the crowd to where the 'Farm chemicals' exhibit was situated.

"Is Tom Allenby here?" he asked the young lady who was manning the counter.

"Mister Allenby? Yes," she replied, but, before she could say any more, Tom Allenby appeared from the rear of the stand.

"As I live and breathe", he exclaimed facetiously, "Now don't tell me anything, let me guess", he placed a hand to his forehead, "You are Oliver Trent, salesman extraordinaire, and you've come today to buy me a whopping great lunch and beg me to give you your old job back".

"Very comical, Tom, ha-ha", said Oliver. "For a start, I wouldn't want my old job back with your lot, I'm doing very nicely thank you, besides, rumour has it that you're heading down the pan, rapidly".

"Don't believe all you hear Ollie, we're not doing too bad. Now what about lunch? On you?"

"Come off it Tom. I'm OK, but I'm only a poor relation compared to you, a miserable rep. What are you now? Chairman? President?"

"Managing Director my friend, and look at me, still got to do my stint on the exhibit here. Come in anyway, I'll buy you a drink"

"No", Oliver declined firmly, "You come with me, there's plenty to drink on my stand and besides, I want you to meet a chappie who I think could put something interesting your way."

"I'm all for that", said Tom, "Let's go".

After a long discussion with the Arab, Tom Allenby was almost a very satisfied man.

"And the result is guaranteed? Whenever this potion is used?"

Ben Acate nodded eagerly.

"You buy, yes?"

"Oh yes", Allenby nodded, "I think we will buy. Tomorrow you travel to London with me".

The following day, Tariq, having spent his time going from airports to railway stations, from stations to bus-depots, sank to his knees on the crowded concourse at Euston and gave thanks to Allah.

He ignored the astonished stares of the

passers-by as he uttered a prayer of gratitude for at last delivering the thief Ben Acate into his hands. He stood up, yes; the fugitive himself had just alighted from the train, and, in the company of another man was walking towards the exit...

Tariq followed.

Chapter 2

Andrew Craig wiped nervously at his spectacles with a handkerchief, replaced them on his nose, then carefully re-read the memo that had caused him such agitation.

The words blurred as he focussed on the initials at the bottom of the flimsy paper, 'H.W', A flamboyant scrawl that could only have been inscribed by Sir Humphrey Wonnacott, the chairman of 'Farm Chemicals Limited' in whose London, Park Royal building, Andrew, as a very junior accountant, occupied the tiniest of offices.

All sorts of possibilities as to why the memo had been sent to him ran through his mind as he stared at the portrait of Sir Humphrey that almost filled one wall of his office. A portrait that had it's fellows on nearly every other wall in the building. In fact, it was said that even the basement car-park had it's one special reproduction of Sir Humphrey's noble features, but Andrew could not swear to that. He's never learnt to drive, so found it unnecessary to ever visit the echoing cavern that housed the vehicles of the favoured few.

Andrew looked at his watch, 'nine-fifteen'.

The memo read 'nine-thirty', panic rose within him. He should be moving. Taking out an inhaler, he breathed deeply as he endeavoured to compose himself, then rising from his seat, passed through the even tinier ante-room that housed Miss Emily Lang, the secretary who, according to the edicts of 'Farm Chemicals' was allocated to three other employees, who , like Andrew, were not entitled to a secretary of their own.

"Meeting with the chairman Miss Lang, I don't know when I'll be back".

He reddened as she looked at him, he always did. Women cast a disturbing influence on him ever since he was a youth, and Emily Lang was no exception. She sat there, her Amazonian frame dwarfing the typewriter on her desk, and nodded silently, but her eyes assessed him as he walked by her.

Twenty-five years of age, unmarried, she'd

found that out. Good-looking? some might not think so, regular features, hair combed straight back. A bit on the short side really, five foot five? Maybe six, and that limp. She shook her head compassionately, the limp, an exaggerated consequence of some childhood fracture, made Andrew Craig, when walking fast, bob up and down like some disjointed puppet. Not the image of desire that a romantic fiction magazine would describe for it's readership, especially with the asthma as well, but, Emily Lang smiled at some inner thought, then continued sorting the morning's mail as the door closed behind the object of her secret longing.

Taking the lift to the eighth floor, Andrew made his way along a thickly carpeted corridor towards the great man's domain. Opening a glass-panelled door, he introduced himself to the young lady he found in the outer office. "Oh yes, Mister Craig" she smiled provocatively and , throwing back her luxuriant blonde hair, leaned back in the chair and exhibited two points of attraction that would have done justice to any centre-fold pin up.

"You can go straight in, they're waiting".

A button on her blouse popped open and Andrew blushed redly, averted his eyes from her exposed cleavage, and, muttering strangled thanks, made to sidle past her desk.

Then, he stumbled, his leg gave way and sent him sprawling. Grabbing desperately to save himself, he pulled over a side table. Papers cascaded about him. The girl reached out and found her arm gripped by his other hand, Andrew pulled hard, instinctively, and the unfortunate lady came forcibly from her chair, bringing with her the telephone and other assorted desktop items which added to the litter as she took Andrew's breath away by landing flat on his stomach.

"Oof" his gasp was lost in her startled scram then, the slamming of a door penetrated his fuddled brain as he stared horrified through the lattice-work of blonde hair that framed his face up into the bearded visage that glared down at the two of them, the chairman!

Sir Humphrey indicated a possible royal lineage by turning a majestic shade of purple then, using what for him seemed to be an impossible degree of self-control, snarled through clenched teeth.

"Just what in God's name do you think you are doing"?

"Er, er, Sir, an accident", Andrew stammered the words, "Please sir, I'm Craig, er....Sir..." his voice trailed off.

"Hmmph!" an explosive sound then, carefully enunciated "well Mister Craig, when you've quite finished cavorting with Lorraine, Miss Johnson, my secretary, I would appreciate your attendance at my little meeting".

Andrew stare fixedly up at the chairman's thick red lips moving deliberately in the mass of black hair surrounding them then suddenly realised that he was still holding tightly to Miss Johnson's struggling body. A body whose rounded form, whose warmth and softness was doing something to his senses, he felt a stirring, an indescribable urge of...

With a startled gasp he almost threw the girl from him and tried to scramble to his feet as Sir Humphrey continued in a voice dripping with unconcealed sarcasm

"By all means finish what you are doing

though"

The door closed abruptly behind the chairman as he went into the inner office. Andrew helped Miss Johnson to her feet,

"What can I say? I'm sorry, are you all right? I'll pick these up", he began to gather the scattered documents.

"No, please", her voice sounded shaky. He continued his flustered efforts, "Stop it", the words, almost screamed, halted him in mid action. He stared. The girl, recovering her composure, smiled.

"Sorry I shouted, but you go in, I'll clear this up"

"Are you sure", Andrew hesitated. She nodded, "Well" said Andrew, then spying his fallen spectacles among the debris, picked them up and put them in his pocket,

"For er reading" he stuttered, "I ...the glasses, you know"?

Lorraine nodded.

"Yes" she said, "Now please Mister Craig, go, they really are waiting for you".

Brushing an ineffectual hand across his rumpled hair and tugging his shirt and jacket straight, Andrew forced a sickly grin, tapped at the office door, and limped swiftly into the other room.

"Aah!" the booming exclamation made him flinch and he stood quaking as Sir Humphrey Rounded his desk and approached him.

As the chairman lifted a hand, Andrew almost cowered, but Sir Humphrey merely took his arm and led him to a chair.

"Sit down! the bearded mouth ordered, then taking a seat opposite, "So, you're Craig eh?"

"Sir? Yes, I'm Craig".

Sir Humphrey laughed,

"Steady on now, no need to be nervous, you, er, you know my secretary then?"

"Indeed no sir", Andrew was indignant, "It was an accident, I fell, stumbled, she, well, she..."

"All right", the chairman leaned forward and patted Andrew's knee. "Nuff said, you married?"

Andrew shook his head, wondering where this was leading.

"How long have you been working for the company?"

Andrew did a quick calculation and replied,

"Ever since, well, it's six, no seven, er..."
"My God man", Sir Humphrey sitting back in his chair and actually snorting, glared at him. "Six years, Seven years? I don't want it exactly, never mind" he shook his head despairingly and his beard waggled as he continued.
"Now Craig, I need your help"
Sir Humphrey took out a cigar case and offered it to Andrew.
"Smoke?"
"No thank you Sir", Andrew tried to smile but only managed an awkward glance as Sir Humphrey returned the case without taking one himself.
"Bad habit anyway", he said brusquely, "could kill you", then taking the case out again, he removed a cigar, lit it and blew a cloud of evil-smelling smoke in Andrew's face. "Got to die sometime though eh"?
Andrew spluttered his agreement through the acrid haze then took out his inhaler and turned away as he operated it.
"What's that? Sir Humphrey asked sharply, "Drugs?"
"No Sir, it's an inhaler, for asthma, I don't use

it very often".

"Oh", said the chairman, his interest waned, "as long as it doesn't interfere with your work eh?"

Then as Andrew made to speak, he lifted a hand in an imperious gesture

"No, that's it. No more chit-chat, to business Craig, now this is what I want you to do".

Andrew listened with growing dismay as the chairman laid out his intentions.

"But Sir", he interjected at one point.

Sir Humphrey looked stonily at him,

"What is it" he asked, "don't you understand anything I've said?"

"Sir, Yes I think so, but..." Andrew was nonplussed, then "I'm an accountant sir!"

"Forgive me Craig", Sir Humphrey said bitingly "But I know you're a bloody accountant, just why do you think you're here? If I wanted a chemist I'd get a chemist and", his tone became menacing, "If I wanted a jumped up Abyssinian rain dancers brolly I'd lay my hands on one of those. Now listen, and listen well, I don't want any slip-ups, got it"?

Thoroughly cowed, Andrew listened.

"So", stated Sir Humphrey, puffing at his cigar, "You got with this Arab gent, collect a phial of", he waved his hand, "Of whatever, and take it to our plant in Essex, follow me?"

Andrew nodded and Sir Humphrey continued "You like working for the company?"

Andrew nodded again, "And no doubt you'd like to continue working?"

Again a nod

"Well Craig you carry out this little task and I can see you going far in Farm Chemicals, he smiled, "You see Albert", Andrew thought about correcting him but remained silent as the chairman went on, "The reason you are being asked to do this service for the company is , well, it's a trifle delicate, but as you probably know, there's a takeover bid in the offing and some of us at Farm Chemicals are thinking seriously of entering the market with a different product, and you?" he made an expansive gesture, "you my boy could be in on the ground floor of any new development",

He stood, and Andrew hastily followed suit "Be in the car park at six-thirty this evening, don't let me down."

"No sir", blurted Andrew, "I won't let you down"

"Bravo Mister Craig" the voice came from behind him and he turned swiftly.

"What, Who?"

Sir Humphrey chuckled

"Allow me Craig, or can I call you Alfred?"

Again Andrew considered a correction but decided against it. He studied the man who had spoken, this must be the Arab. The chairman continued,

"Meet Ben, er Acate, right?"

Andrew took in the height of the man, about six feet tall, aged about thirty he reckoned, though the swarthiness of his features made it difficult to tell. The hawk-like face turned to Sir Humphrey as the chairman spoke and Andrew saw the glitter in his eyes as he hung onto the words avidly. If only, Andrew thought, the Arab was not wearing an ordinary suit, he would have been the picture of what a desert-dweller should look like.

'Everybody's Arab' Andrew smiled as the idea ran through his mind and then was nudged, forcibly, by Sir Humphrey.

"Are you listening Craig"?

Hastily Andrew assured him that he was. "Right, as I was saying, you take this man to his home, pick up the phial, and, mark this well. Do not let the potion out of your sight until you actually hand it over to whoever's at the factory. I think it's a Doctor Bryant, so that's who you deal with. Got it?"

Andrew nodded excitedly and his mind raced as he thought of the Arab's home. He could picture the burning sands, the exotic scents of the desert in bloom. Bedouin, lazy nights amid the palm-shrouded oasis. He was disturbed from his reverie by Sir Humphrey.

"Ben Acate will meet you in the car park this evening. I'll be there to see you off. I understand from my managing director that a leave of absence has been arranged for you. Oh, and here's your expenses".

Andrew took the proffered envelope. "A hundred pounds "Then the chairman's voice became sharper

"Now Craig, get this chappy home, pick up the goods, then it's down to Essex and deliver them o.k.?"

"Yes indeed sir", Andrew's senses were reeling

"I think I understand but sir, a hundred pounds? Will that be enough sir, I mean, Africa, Arabia?"

Sir Humphrey cut him short,

"What the blazes are you going on about? Arabia? I want you to take Ben Acate home to Bradford and then to the fertilizer factory in Essex, Do you understand?"

The thundering finality of the chairman's closing question made Andrew literally quake in his shoes, muttering a strong of "yes sirs" he left the office and scuttled away down the corridor with an up and down motion that made a couple of young office-girls titter behind their cupped hands as he sped past them.

No one in the corridor noticed the dark-featured man who slipped quietly from the door of Sir Humphrey's adjoining suite and walked innocently away...

Chapter 3

"What a berk!" sir Humphrey muttered "Tom Allenby scraped the bottom of the barrel when he picked him for this job"
"Pardon, what is this berk that you speak of"? The chairman laughed.
"Take no notice old chap. I was only commenting on our friend Craig".
"You do not trust him?"
Sir Humphrey snorted "of course I trust him, he won't do anything amiss, or he better not, "he finished in a vicious tone.
"Pardon"
"Pardon, my tall hat", the chairman mouthed, then aloud "you see Ben,"
"Acate El idi asa Yalef..." the Arab interjected then was interrupted in turn as the chairman said harshly, "Shush don't burble", he glanced up at the portrait of himself that hung on the wall and unconsciously adopted the same pose as the Arab stroking his aquiline nose, said

! A thousand pardons oh illustrious ..."

"And cut that out, flannel doesn't wash with me"

Ben Acate nodded silently, though his swarthy face darkened even more and his eyes glittered dangerously.

At that moment there was a tap at the door and on the chairman's shouted command it opened and the blonde secretary entered.

"Excuse me sir, Mister Allenby"

"About time, come in Tom, come in" he moved across and grasped the hand of the man who had entered. I'm glad you are here, you know Ben Doodah don't you"?

Allenby nodded.

"Of course, I sent him to you, what's up Humphrey, getting forgetful in your old age?

"Forgetful? Maybe, look at me Tom, I'm the chairman of this whole shebang and I'm nervous. Look at my hands, "he waved them frantically up and down, "and what about Craig? You picked a right character there didn't you?"

"Calm yourself Humphrey," Tom Allenby smiled placatingly and sat opposite the shaken chairman.

"Don't tell me that. I am bloody calm, it's just," the chairman lit another cigar, "Well, it's ...Oh look here Tom, you're my managing director, my friend, you've got your fingers in everything, Are we doing the right thing trying to get this..." he paused, "This ...What the hell are we getting anyway"?

Tom Allenby smiled.

"The details are in the folder I sent you, but", he sighed theatrically "I'll tell you again, now are we sitting comfortably"?

"No need to be facetious", the chairman said "Hang on though, " he spoke to Miss Johnson who was still in the room "Lorraine my dear, take this gentleman and give him a cup of tea or something", he indicated the Arab with a nod of his head then said, looking straight at him "You won't mind waiting outside will you? This'll only take a minute"

The Arab glared, but allowed himself to be led from the office by Sir Humphrey's secretary.

"That's it", exclaimed the chairman, then taking a key from his desk drawer, opened a cabinet, Brandy Tom?"

"It's a bit early but go on then, make mine a large one"

Sir Humphrey poured the drinks, picked his smouldering cigar from the ashtray and took a despairing puff at it.

"Now this bloody thing wont draw, what a day!" Tom Allenby eyed his brimming glass tentatively, took a cautious sip, then setting it carefully on the desk-top said,

"I can see you haven't put your hand in your pocket for this one Humphrey, I'd probably only get a damp glass if you were paying for it".

"That's funny Tom, really funny. Thank the Lord I can still give a glass of brandy, if the government had it their way it'd be water in the hospitality cabinet, and that'd be rationed"

"All the same Humphrey, it's wasteful", Tom drank again, "But it's nice eh?"

"Aye" agreed the chairman, "Now let's go through this again, and convince me that it's worth the effort".

"Of course it is .It's going to be worth a great deal of money too". Tom Allenby leaned forward earnestly "Look here Humphrey; it's been very nice playing round with Nitrates and

Phosphates, and every other kind of 'phates' that we normally deal in. But this is different, a scent, a basic aroma that will facilitate the mating of any animal you care to think of." Hr took another sip of his brandy "Just think what we'd have missed if that Arab chappy had gone to I.C.I. or one of the other fertiliser companies".

"What fertiliser companies?" asked Sir Humphrey petulantly, "I don't know much chemistry, and I haven't got a clue when it comes to Phosphates of any description, but I know there aren't many fertiliser companies nowadays, not independent ones like us, and we won't be around for long if this scheme of yours doesn't work".

"Trust me", said Tom.

"Oh I do old friend, I do. Don't forget though, I don't bother too much about being clued up on what we sell, but I know quite a lot when it comes to money", he nodded sagely then asked, "But what about Craig? How come you chose a chap like that to..."

"To take charge of everything, think about it Humphrey, "Tom exhorted, "An accountant, nothing to do with production, just a junior man in the accounts department. He goes to Bradford, brings back the stuff, we analyse it, produce it ourselves and, if anything goes wrong? Away goes Craig. If all goes well? "He tapped a finger against the side of his nose, "We could even form another company on the strength of anticipated demand"

"Will we get demand?"

"Of course", Tom beamed "Every farmer in the country will want some once they hear about it"

Sir Humphrey rubbed his hands,

"Good, good , you've convinced me, and this way, if it turns out ok, well no-one on the board needs to know do they?"

"Just between us Humphrey".

The two men clinked glasses and toasted the expected success of their venture.

Emily Lang was disappointed. In fact she even felt cheated, for since her and Andrew had become, if not friends, then friendly acquaintances, she had used every opportunity to touch him , to show him in whatever way she could that she was more than interested in him and now? Her disappointment was heartfelt when she took in his morning coffee and found the office empty. 'Where was he', was his absence due to the mysterious summons from the chairman? Then she chided herself, surely there was nothing wrong, she was acting like an infatuated adolescent rather than a woman of twenty-eight, but Andrew? Well no other man had ever raised such strong emotions in her.

Perhaps he had been sacked. She shuddered as the notion ran through her mind, and such desolation came over her that, as the door opened and in he walked she couldn't contain herself. Throwing her arms wide, she clasped him to her ample bosom,

"Oh, "she gasped "you're here".

"I say," he uttered in a muffled voice, "Miss Lang, Emily, please, whatever…"

She released him abruptly; her face red with shame and Andrew's a vivid crimson as he sought to catch his breath after the brief suffocation between her generous breasts.

"I'm sorry Andrew, I shouldn't, its only," she lowered her gaze and mumbled coyly, "I thought you'd been fired or something, and I well..I" she reached a tentative hand towards him and Andrew, trying vainly to use his inhaler, stepped out of reach hastily, caught the back of his legs against the desk, knocked over the coffee that Emily had placed there and sat in the resultant puddle.

Leaping up, he tried to pull the clinging wetness of his trousers away from his skin and as Emily tried to help, he turned away. She stepped to face him, he turned again, and they twisted around like participants in some weird dance until she caught a hand in his belt, pulled him to a stop and said,

"Please, take them off, I'll dry them, I'll ..." she started to undo his flies, he grabbed her hands.

"No, go away Emily; leave me alone, just..."

"What's going on?" the peremptory bark of the chairman's voice halted them in their movements and they stood transfixed. Emily's hand on his half-open zipper and he grasping her wrist.

"Craig!" the word was spat out, then the chairman's tone softened as he continued with a note of wonder in his voice, "How do you do it Craig> Are you a raving sex maniac or something?" he shook his head slowly, "Is this I pay you for? This debauchery during office hours".

"S, Sir," Andrew stuttered, "S, S, Sir, you don't understand".

"Don't you try to justify this," Sir Humphrey hissed, "I understand all right, I don't believe it, but I can see with my own eyes what's going on. My God man…" lost for words, he stood for a moment, then, with a strangled exclamation, left the room.

"See what you've done?" Andrew rounded on Emily.

"I'm sorry", she said, "But he's gone now, take off your trousers, I won't look". She turned on heel and went out, saying as she did so, "I'll get you some fresh coffee and you can tell me what's been happening".

Sir Humphrey Wonnacott returned to his office

and asked his secretary,

"Has Mister Allenby gone out?"

"Only to his own office sir, He took the Arab gentleman with him, shall I call him?"

"No thanks", said the chairman, "I'll walk round and see him".

The managing director's office was on the same floor as his so it only took a minute to walk the few paces to his door, give a perfunctory tap and go in.

"Hello Humphrey", Tom Allenby looked up as he entered, then seeing the stricken look on the chairman's face, asked, "Trouble".

The chairman shrugged, sat down next to Ben Acate and said

"You tell me Tom, I've just caught that Craig again, and what do you think?"

As Sir Humphrey related what he had seen in Craig's office, tom Allenby chuckled,

"Is that all? Why the man sounds as if he's just a red-blooded male, mind you", he reflected, "He didn't give that impression when I chose him for this job".

Humphrey sighed.

"I don't know Tom; I hope it goes well for us".

"It will", Allenby assured him, "Stop worrying about Craig and think about the money".
"What about my money honoured sirs?"
The Arab's question brought both men's eyes to focus on him, then Sir Humphrey said, "Don't you worry, Abou Ben whatsit, you'll get your money".

The time was creeping up to six-fifteen as Andrew placed his spectacles in the top pocket of his jacket and went into the secretary's office.
"Hello", he said as he saw Emily, "Working overtime?"
She smiled.
"No", then seriously, "I've been thinking about what you told me. This trip, mysterious isn't it?"
"Not really," replied Andrew, "Like I said, Sir Humphrey wants to keep it quiet, special treatment. I…"
She cut him short.
"It could be you who's in for some special treatment"

"Why" he commented, "What could be wrong with a trip to Bradford? And then Essex? That village..." a worried look spread over his face. Emily asked what the matter was,

"The village, "he replied, "I don't know where it is. Sir Humphrey will think I'm a proper idiot, I can't remember the name can you?"

Emily smiled.

"Of course, I bring you their invoices twice each week".

"That's right," Andrew breathed, "Whitley Warren, by Tilbury isn't it?"

"See, you do know", said Emily, then shrugging, "I don't know how long they'll be there though, they never handle a lot of business".

"No", Andrew agreed, "The overseas stuff comes into Swansea under licence, and gets processed there as well".

Emily came round the desk,

"I suppose you've got to go now?"

He reddened again; silly really, surely no man who sat with a woman when he was trouser less could be embarrassed? But he certainly was.

She reached out and touched his cheek, "Please Emily, d...d...don't", he stuttered, she laughed;

"Listen to old worrier now, I'm not going to hurt you", she looked over his shoulder at the clock, "Hadn't you better be going?"

He turned and saw the time, then panicked, "It's, oh, look at the time, I've got to go, the lift", he almost ran out of the room, his voice trailing off behind him,

"Does the lift go to the basement?"

"Yes", Emily cried, following him from the office and keeping pace as he sped to the lifts.

One came almost immediately and he disappeared into the depths.

Emily considered the situation for a short moment then fetching her handbag, she took the next lift down...

Chapter 4

At six-thirty precisely Andrew Craig stepped from the lift into the basement and saw Sir Humphrey Wonnacott standing by the side of a large black limousine with Ben Acate.

Walking over, he said brightly,

"Good evening sir, I'm here"

"Not only a fool, but a master of understatement" answered the chairman.

Andrew ignored the remark but said "Hello", in reply to the Arab's greeting.

"Right Craig", Sir Humphrey brought his attention to the moment "Time to go". Then to Ben Acate "If you get in the car, my man will take you to Bradford", he laughed, "Quicker you get there the quicker you get back eh?"

Ben Acate opened the passenger door; Andrew nodded his thanks and made to enter.

The Arab stooped to get in at the same time and they collided, bumping heads.

Sir Humphrey stared at the two of them groaning, and asked,

"What are you doing?"

"Doing sir?" replied Craig

"Yes, bloody doing you cretin, D.O.I.N.G. What are you up to?"

Andrew rubbed his head, stared at the chairman, then indicated the car.

"I'm getting in the car, sir, you told me I'm to go to Bradford with this man."

"Taking him you fool, taking him"

Sir Humphrey snatched at the driver's door handle, breaking a manicured finger-nail as he did so.

"Now look what you've done"! The car door slammed open "In", he pointed a quivering finger, "And get yourself and Ben Acate to Bradford".

The Arab thanked Sir Humphrey and got in the rear seat, but Andrew stood silent

"Now what's the matter?" asked the chairman.

From somewhere Andrew found the courage to answer,

"I can't drive sir", he whispered, then louder, "I can't drive".

Sir Humphrey's visage whitened, flushed through a rather attractive pink, to a blaze of scarlet, then a deep shade of plum as he spoke.

"You can't drive, can't drive?" he began to pace the floor and his voice rose "I don't believe this, I do not bloody believe it, someone tell me it's not happening please", his eyes sought the ceiling "If there's anyone at all up there, tell me I'm dreaming", suddenly a movement caught his eye and he turned to face Emily Lang who was approaching from the direction of the lifts, "Who are you?" he barked.

"Emily", Andrew called, thankful for the sight of a friendly face.

"Oh yes", Sir Humphrey nodded, "I remember", he waved a hand towards Andrew, "you and him, in his office".

"I'm his secretary Sir", Emily said sternly.

"I don't care what you are woman, can you drive?"

"Of course sir".

"Well get in this bloody vehicle and get this pair to Bradford quick as you like"

As if in a trance, Emily got in the car, started the engine, and with a grating of gears that brought an unintelligible outburst from the chairman, slowly moved away.

The three people in the car were silent as the limousine emerged from the car-park and filtered into the stream of traffic that filled the darkening streets.

Suddenly Emily broke the silence.

"Could you tell me where I'm going"?

The two men, until then sitting quietly in the back seat of the car, staring out of their respective windows, swung their heads simultaneously, looked at each other, then at the back of Emily's head.

Andrew caught her eye in the rear-view mirror and said,

"Er, Bradford, yes?" he directed the question at the Arab who nodded his agreement.

They continued their journey then suddenly; Emily applied the brakes, swung the wheel hard over, and skidded to a halt as the tyres banged roughly against the kerb.

Ben Acate sprawled across the seat, his mouth open and a stream of guttural Arabic turning the air blue. Andrew's face flattened against the front passenger seat and he groaned nasally.

"What happened?" then he stared in amazement. Emily was cursing softly and keeping time with her words by banging a clenched fist against the steering wheel.

"What?" Andrew began again, "Emily are you ..."

She turned a threatening gaze on him and he pushed back into the confines of his seat.

"You asked what?" her voice crackled as she spoke, "It's me who should be asking, Just what are we doing anyway? How come I'm driving to Bradford, or anywhere for that matter? Who said that you or I must go away?" Andrew sought for an answer.

"Why", he offered "The chairman is..." she continued as if he hadn't spoken,

"The chairman told you to go with this man. Who's the chairman to say what you do out of working hours?", then her tone softened. "Look Andrew, have you been home? Have you told your landlady that you're going away?" then as he shook his head, "How long are you going to be? What's it in aid of?"

Once again he shook his head, her words echoing inside his brain, she was right of course, what was he doing? He stared at Emily in some bewilderment, then,

"I've had no tea" he commented.

She stared at him, her mouth working frantically s she struggled for words, then , straining hard against an overpowering urge to scream, Emily forced a sickly smile and said fondly,

"Oh Andrew…"

"Pardon", Ben Acate said, "Are we not going to my home now?" he sounded puzzled, "should we not collect the potion?" his lip trembled,

"Sir Humphrey will not pay me if I do not return with it Aieeee", he wailed.

"Shut up," Emily rounded on him, "Stupid man, don't you think we've got things to worry about?"

Ben Acate fell silent, but his eyes spoke volumes as he stared at Emily.

"Well?" asked Andrew, "Do we go to Bradford or what?"

"Yes", Ben Acate said forcefully.

"Silence" ordered Emily, equally as strong, then, "Yes, we'll go to Bradford, but not before we get organised, and not before we sort things out with Sir Humphrey".
Andrew let the words sink into his befuddled brain then said in an agitated fashion,
"Emily? Is er", he saw she was about to speak and rushed on, "I mean, Sir Humphrey, the chairman, I don't think I could, well, you know, talk to him properly like, it's just..."
"Andrew", her tone was sharp, "He's only a man, the same as you are, it's about time somebody told him where to go anyway".
Andrew pouted.
"He may be only a man, but he's our boss. Can't we see him when we get back?"
She looked scathingly at him, was this man she knew? Liked? Even. She sighed, loved?
"All right Andrew "she said resignedly, "We'll got to Bradford"
Starting the engine of the car, she swung it into the traffic, then said, "But the first café we come to, the first telephone, we're stopping, we're eating and we're telling someone where it is we are going, right?"

Andrew let her words wash over him, they were moving, everything was going to be all right, it was warm inside the car, he stifled a yawn then, murmuring "Of course, of course", he settled himself in the back seat, beamed at the reflection of Emily's eyes in the mirror, smiled at Ben Acate, then letting his eyes close, began to utter a series of soft, snoring noises...

The headlights of the dark-coloured car that travelled behind them lit up the interior, but Andrew didn't notice, he slept.

The chairman sat behind his desk, the brandy from the hospitality cabinet going down very nicely and the smoke from the cigar curling in the gloom of his unlit office.

A relaxing moment, yet Sir Humphrey was perturbed. His experience in the basement car-park had unsettled him, although he took solace in the fact that he had a least set in motion the wheels that would, with any luck, turn full circle and deliver fortune into his lap. He looked at his watch, switched the desk lamp on to see better, then jumped, startled, as the phone rang shrilly. A blaze of anger against the unfortunate secretary that had had the temerity to allow the call to come through to his office, the n just as suddenly receded as he realised that the time was past seven pm and everybody had long since gone home. He picked up the receiver.

"Hello"

"Ah Humphrey, at last"

"Tom, is that you?"

"Yes, Everything all right?"

"Of course, except for..." he launched into an account of the evening's events, finishing, "I tell you tom , I could have died when he told me he couldn't drive, Oh and that reminds me, I've given his secretary leave as well...I had to.."

"No Problem Humphrey, we'll sort that out tomorrow, now I think you should be giving some thought to our next move. Obviously you'll be called on to resign at the shareholders meeting and.." he wasn't allowed to finish, as the chairman roared,

"What the hell do you mean, resign? From my own company? That's ridiculous"

Tom made placatory noises then said quietly, "Not so ridiculous Humphrey", then as the chairman attempted to speak" No listen, I know it's your company, in name anyway, but unfortunately you're not in any position to dictate. Your only hope is to preach diversification, you know, when you address the shareholders and convince them that this new product is going to make them all rich".
"But Tom, I thought we were going to handle this ourselves?" the chairman sounded puzzled.
"I'm the major shareholder anyway, there'll be no need for preaching, I can push through whatever I like"
"Because you're the chairman?" Tom chuckled. "No, you've been watching too much television. The board take notice of the shareholders because they, collectively, own the majority. Cast your mind back, think of what we've been going through, the premises we let go to obtain working capital, why, the building you're sitting in now is only rented. In Seventy-two our cargoes were held up in the Suez, remember? You sold off your largest block of

shares to pay our way while that lot was going on. Well you never did get them back you know.

Take a look at our figures this year so far, we've..."

Sir Humphrey interjected.

"Maybe, but we're not broke yet are we? Our share prices are healthy".

"You're as broke as you'll ever be. Share prices are good, very good, what I'm telling you id that you don't own any".

Tom began to catalogue further possible calamities but the chairman interrupted harshly.

"All right , all right" , he fell silent the reality of what tom Allenby was saying sinking into his mind and making him feel for the first time in his life, unsure, vulnerable even, then attempting to throw off this totally foreign emotion , he asked softly,

"You're on my side though Tom?"

"Of course", Tom replied, "And what's more, with what I've got on some of our compatriots, the board might be telling you what to do, but I'll be telling the board, "He chuckled again, "I bet you're drinking to the success of our venture eh?"

"Well, I am having a drink".

"Good, have one for me as well, for this time next week we'll either have Farm Chemicals on top of the heap again, or we'll have our own private company manufacturing the new mating aid. I tell you Humphrey, we can't lose". Sir Humphrey commented in a woebegone voice, "just as long as the heap isn't a pile of our own fertiliser and we sink in it without a trace."

Laughing heartily, tom Allenby bid him a pleasant good night and rang off.

The car bearing Ben Acate and Andrew turned into the slip road leading to 'Four mile Service Area', and as Emily slowed and bumped carefully over the concrete mounds that were in the approach road, the slight jolts woke Andrew. He stretched in the confines of the back seat, stared blankly at the back of Emily's head, glanced sideways at the Arab, then rubbed a hand across the steamed up window and peered into the darkness of the night.

"Is this Bradford? Are we here?"

The car eased to a stop outside the lighted front of the restaurant, Emily switched off the engine and turned to Andrew.

"We are here", she said, "But it's not Bradford, It's Four Mile Services, though four miles from where I haven't got a clue. The last town was Luton, and according to the signs Northampton is still eighteen miles away. But don't let that bother you. Let's get something to eat, all right?"

Andrew and Ben Acate clambered from the car and followed Emily into the restaurant. Spotting a toilet, Andrew excused himself and made a beeline for it. He stood relieving himself as Ben Acate followed him in and hovered nearby. Self-consciously, he finished and tidied himself as he asked,

"Did you want something?"

The Arab smiled.

"I'm sorry Mister Craig sir, I didn't mean to embarrass you by watching, I just wanted to say..."

"Yes".

"The lady", Ben Acate moved his hands to describe a woman's shape in the air, "She is well-built, her breasts, her hips, she could have many children," he paused, "Is she your woman?"

Andrew blushed fiercely. He had never thought of Emily in that way, but, as his mouth was forming words that would put the Arab in his place, he inwardly felt a surge of, what was it, affection? Love? Maybe raw passion? He shuddered and said sternly,

"I don't think that is any of your business, and anyway, it's not the sort of thing that I'd care to discuss with anyone"

"Peace Mister Craig..." the Arab waved a laconic hand, "It's only that if you yourself are not intending to take the lady, then I will".

"You will not"! Stated Andrew emphatically, "That's disgusting, ugh", he turned and stalked from the toilet to where Emily waited.

"I've bought cups of tea for the moment", she greeted him, "Do you want a hot meal? Cos if you do, you'll have to pay out of the firm's hundred pounds, I haven't got much in my handbag, I'll need money for petrol anyway,

"then seeing his face, "What's up Andrew?"
"Nothing "he snapped, then contritious, "Sorry Emily, but it's that Arab, he's..." Andrew considered what to say, "Well he made a remark about you", he sat down, "I didn't like it at all!"

She smiled fondly and asked what the remark had been.

"Nothing", he repeated firmly.

"Oh well," Emily spotted Ben Acate, "I'll ask him myself"

As the Arab arrived, he touched Emily lightly on the shoulder and said,

"I see you have provided refreshments ma Cherie".

Emily looked up.

"Ma cherie?" you speak French.

"Oui", Ben Acate leered at her, "C'est ma deuxieme langue, L'une pour les femmes", then he whispered in her ear, "Et l'amour".

'Quite so', Emily pulled her head away quickly, "It may be your second language but, I'm not one of your femmes, and you can forget any thought of love, so just sit down and drink your tea".

"Yes", spat Andrew, who was valiantly sieving his knowledge of schoolboy French to understand what the Arab had said, "Finis Monsieur, er, Sil vous plait", he added triumphantly, then , moving his chair closer to that of Emily, he sat proudly, defying any further approach from Ben Acate.

The Arab shrugged and took his place at the table.

Emily, after they had been sitting for a half-hour or so, asked Andrew for money.

"I'll get some petrol", she said, "you two finish eating and I'll call you when we're ready to go". The men nodded and continued their meal.

Within twenty minutes Emily returned.

"Bad news", she sat down, "You'll never credit this, the car's had it. Something to do with the carburettor, they can't fix it till the morning".

"What are we going to do?" asked Andrew.

Ben Acate scowled darkly.

"We must do something, my money is at stake" Emily tutted.

"Money, is that all you can think about? What about me and Andrew? What are we supposed to do?"

They sat for a moment then,

"I know", the men looked at Emily as she spoke, "this is a motel, if you, Ben Acate finish your journey by bus, then Andrew and I could take rooms for the night, You go home , pick up your bits and pieces, whatever it is you're fetching, and we'll meet here in the morning and carry on to Essex, right?"

"A bus?" Ben Acate sounded puzzled, "How could I get a bus at this hour?"

"To Bradford!" Emily's eyes brightened,

"Why, when I found the car had troubles, I asked the mechanic, there's a bus stop just outside the restaurant, apparently the driver gets something to eat…"

"Ah, but at what time?" asked Ben Acate.

"Ten 'o' clock", replied Emily promptly,

"Andrew will pay the fare, it's simple. The same bus returns in the morning, you'll be on it, we all go to Essex…" her eyes met Andrew's a he swivelled his head from her to Ben Acate as they spoke, "what do you think?"

"Well, whatever you say Emily, but shouldn't we go with Mister Acate?"

"No" said Emily sharply, "besides, three return

fares would cost too much, you've only got a hundred pounds you know".

"Yes I suppose you're right, "he agreed, "how much do you want?" he asked Ben Acate.

The man waved his hands,

"Ask Miss Emily, she appears to have all the information".

The fronds of a nearby potted palm rustled and fell into place as a pair of watching eyes disappeared behind them, Tariq, the Sheikh's eldest son was puzzled, but deciding, he left the restaurant and sat in his car, waiting for Ben Acate to board the bus. Soon he must have the potion...

That evening Andrew lay on the bed in his room and sighed wearily. His eyelids fluttered, then closed as a feeling of lassitude spread through his body and it was as if his ears were filled with cotton-wool for he almost missed the opening and closing of the door and Emily asking,

"Tired, Andrew?"

He smiled sleepily, "I am rather, still, he

started to sit up, "Time for supper?"

"Not yet", she replied, pushing him gently back onto the bed, "there's plenty of time". Andrew suppressed a gasp of astonishment as he felt her hand stroking his leg. A tingling sensation grew and threatened to overpower his senses as she became more personal with her touch, her hair fell about his face and her hot breath scorched his parted lips as she lowered her mouth to his.

"Oh Emily", he breathed before the kiss smothered any further attempt at words, bust fingers began to undo the buttons of his shirt and he groaned feelingly as her mobile lips made a tantalising journey from his face, ever so slowly down his exposed chest, then to the soft white flesh of his belly...

Suddenly she stood up, and his eyes widened as his hands involuntarily reached out and sought to restrain her, he made to speak then stopped, slack-jawed as she stripped off her dress, then reached behind her and set free her breasts.

"Emily", his voice was hoarse as he pushed the single word through the dryness of his throat.

She smiled as a sinuous movement served to rid her of her underskirt, her pants, then stood before him completely nude.

Andrew uttered a gurgling moan as he snatched at his own clothes, frantically tearing at the open shirt while at the same time, attempting to divest himself of his trousers, one hand scrabbling for the zipper and the other pulling desperately at his waistband. At last he half-succeeded, wriggled his legs, rolled his body this way and that, and finally fell to the floor with an almighty thud as he went too near the edge of the bed.

He lay, face upwards, his chest heaving then paused mesmerised as Emily Lang came into his field of vision, as she lowered herself gently on top of his prostrate body, and as she folded him tenderly within her arms and pressed him close to those amazing orbs that promised so much...

Andrew couldn't speak, didn't want to speak, but silently, even as she began to transport him to realms of ecstasy he had only ever imagined in the past, his mind reverberated to the echoing, majestic sound of her name...

Emily…

Chapter 5

Fred Alexander, works convenor of the Farm Chemicals processing plant at Whitley Warren, was addressing the Doctor Sydney Bryant, head of the plant, his deputy and senior chemist, Peter Winfield, and the shop steward, Eddy Gates.

"So gentlemen I must officially back Brother Gates in bringing the men out on strike. I know redundancy will be inevitable in the long run but, until I contact my national officers then Brother Gates is right to show the strength of the membership".

Bryant and Winfield stared blankly at him during this oration then transferred their blank looks to each other. Finally Bryant spoke,

"What are you on about Fred?"

"The strike", the convenor replied, "I'm saying the workers have got to show their resistance to redundancies".

"But we haven't got any workers"

"Well", replied Alexander, "Admittedly there's no warehouse staff left, but we've got about six drivers on the transport and ..."

"Wrong Fred", Eddy Gates interrupted him, "the lorries and drivers are contracted out, there's only security", he ticked off his fingers, "Five blokes on nights, maintenance three, and us of course, ten".

"Ten", said Fred Alexander, "And I'm the convenor for ten workers?"

"Say nowt Brother", intoned Doctor Bryant, "And possibly you'll remain convenor, that is", he added, "If London doesn't get wise to the fact that you've got nobody to convene", he became serious, "And that's when the axe will fall".

"You can see that happening?" asked Winfield. "Can't you?" Bryant rose from his chair, they can't continue paying us for doing nothing", he shrugged, "But I'm as much in the dark as anyone".

The shop steward stood abruptly and Fred Alexander shot a questioning glance at him.

"Don't stare Fred", said Eddy Gates, "I've

listened to you all talk and I know you think it's a bit daft, but it's right to have a show of strength."

"I thought we'd settled that", observed Doctor Bryant, "How can we have a show of strength of you haven't the staff to show it?"

Eddy sounded adamant.

"We can still picket the main gate".

Bryant laughed.

"Very fitting, Gates on the gate, eh?"

The others groaned at his flippancy and Winfield asked,

"Why do you want to picket the main gate? It's not been in use for ages".

Eddy Gates thought for a moment.

"It's policy", he said firmly, "union policy, right Brother?" he addressed the question to Fred Alexander who, hurriedly standing also, faced Doctor Bryant and said,

"Er, yes, policy. Probably for a week or two? A token picket".

"Well gentlemen", Bryant went to the door of the office, opened it, and stood there as the others taking the hint, began to file out. "Apart from this being the most stupid action I've heard of for some time, do feel free to picket for as long as you want, now, are we going to the village for lunch?"

Amid a chorus of assent, he closed the door behind them and smiled.

For the tenth time the bus driver snarled through gritted teeth in reply to Ben Acate's question.

"I shan't tell you again mate. The bus will stop at Four Mile service station, it's got to stop cos I'm driving and I want my breakfast", he thumped his fist on the steering wheel. "Now sit down and let me drive this F...God, don't make me swear, sit down", he finished on a crescendo and the Arab couldn't help but feel a slight tremble of apprehension at the busman's tirade. He resumed his seat and stared glumly out of the window.

The scattering of early morning passengers who had been riveted by the bus-driver's choice of phrase and his vehemence in discussing the destination of the vehicle with Ben Acate, continued with their own business of sleeping, reading, and it was maybe one or two of them at the most who noticed that the small black car that had followed them from Bradford, stayed close behind them until now, had, after falling increasingly behind, pulled in at the side of the road, and a rather irate Arab was staring at the receding bus and shaking an ineffectual fist at its rapidly disappearing tail-lights.

Moments before he was actually aware, Andrew's hands were moving, searching for...his eyes opened and he sat upright in the bed.
Emily had gone.
Disappointment flooded his body, he caught a gasping breath and reached automatically for his inhaler, then his hand stopped short as the realisation of what had transpired between Emily and himself struck home.
He stretched luxuriously, almost, purring like a contented tomcat then , for the first time in

what seemed like an eternity, he took unaided, a deep, lung-filling inhalation, closed his eyes, and gave his mind to a re-living of the night...
He was still in his trance-like state when the door opened and the subject of his reverie entered briskly.

"Rise and shine", she said, ignoring his attempt at a sexy smile, "The bus arrived and Ben Acate is in the dining room. Do you want breakfast"?

He leapt from the bed and, swiftly crossing the room, tried to embrace her.

"No time for that Andrew", she said, easily eluding his clutching arms, then she pointed to his bare legs, "No limp? Or is that just when you're in the office?"

"I...er..limp?" he was muttering to the closed door, Emily had left the room.

When Andrew had dressed, he made a rather irregular progress to the motel dining-room because of his looking down at every other step to ascertain whether or not he did limp. On entering, he stood for a moment trying to see where Emily and the Arab were sitting, but she spotted him first and came over.

"Bacon sandwich on the table", he looked in the direction of her pointed finger and saw Ben Acate, "Go sit with your friend, " she said, "I'll buy you a cup of tea".

"He's not my friend", he stated, but too late, she'd gone again, this time to the head of the queue where she ignored the stares and mumbled complaints of the other customers and was served immediately.

After they had eaten, Ben Acate winked knowingly at Andrew and commented slyly, "When the urge rises will the car not work again", Emily coloured fiercely as Andrew mulled over this cryptic remark then the Arab gave a loud guffaw and slapped his back. "Never mind my friend, sometimes a strong woman is a boon, now", he became serious and taking from his pocket a small box, he produced from it a glass bottle about six inches in height. Lowering his voice to a confidential whisper he said, "This Andrew is what your master is going to pay me for. I now give it to you".

Andrew took the bottle and donning his spectacles, held it up to the light,

"What is it ?" he asked, shaking it.

Ben Acate made a warning gesture and pulled his arm down.

"No, " he hissed, "Men could die for the secret of the Khan, hide it quickly".

Andrew gaped at the Arab's intensity.

"What's a Kohani?" he asked.

Ben Acate stood, struck a pose, and stated proudly,

"My people, we are Kohani, the finest camel breeders in the world".

Andrew's mouth dropped even further as he stared.

"Yes", said Emily, unimpressed, "Are we going now, I'd like to continue our journey, you know, finish the job in hand and all that."

The Arab started to move obediently towards the exit, the others rose to follow them , then,

"Hang on a minute Emily", said Andrew "I want to talk to you"

"What about?"

"You know," Andrew essayed a wink, then what passed as a knowing look, Emily stared.

"Andrew, what's the matter with your face?"

Crestfallen, he said,

"Nothing I suppose, but I would have thought, last night, well we did , er…" he reddened, and taking off his spectacles, fussed with them to cover his discomfort.

"Oh Andrew", Emily's voice softened, she gave a quick glance to where the Arab was waiting then kissed him gently. "We will talk" , she whispered. "We will, and more", he shivered as her fingers traced a pattern on his cheek, "But not now Andrew, let's get this job over with and then?" she kissed him again, and Andrew smirked satisfiedly, then almost floating on air, he followed her out of the motel dining-room and got into the back seat of the car with the Arab.

"Whitley Warren?" asked Emily gaily

"Whitley Warren", chorused the men in reply, though for the life of him, Ben Acate didn't have a clue what they were on about.

Chapter 6

The Sheikh of Sheikh's sat before his tent at the oasis of Abu Kohani.

The majority of families had left for the markets and only the most immediate of his tribe remained,

Suddenly the palms started to sway and the surface of the water rippled violently as a helicopter came low over the trees and hovered close to the roofs of the tents before it's pilot landed the machine in the clearing where the Said was seated.

The blades slowed, the engine noise diminished, and as a western dressed Arab emerged from the interior, a circle of the Sheikh's personal guards, armed with rifles, seemed to materialise from nowhere with their weapons at the ready.

"Salaam illustrious one", the suited Arab made a low bow and stood, his head inclined, until the sheikh designed an answer,

"I know you Abdullah Karim, are you not the servant of my brother?"

The man, in fact the most trusted of employees of the Sheikh's relative, Achmed, an oil-rich prince, felt he could now raise his head.

"Yes, exalted one, I have that honour".

The Said beckoned him to approach and signalled the guards to let him through.

"Now" he said, as the man neared him, "Why do you come?"

"A message from England. It was received by telephone, not two hours ago and your brother despatched me to bring it to you".

The Sheikh waved the man closer,

"Well" he asked,

"It is permitted?" the Arab enquired deferentially.

The chief nodded impatiently and listened as the man spoke at length.

"And great one", he added, "I have been instructed to tell you that, although your brother, the Prince, has had to leave for America to discuss another matter, and is then expected in Switzerland by his bankers, whatever is needed for the resolution of your own business will be met by myself and your brother's staff."

The chief nodded as he listened, then rose and indicated that the messenger follow him into his tent.

"Wait", he commanded, then indicated several plates of food placed about the nest of cushions on the richly carpeted floor, "Eat if you wish, I am grateful for my brother's felicitations and have need of perhaps", he hesitated "Transport".

Without further explanation the Sheikh left the tent an returned in a little while with a younger Arab clad in the traditional burnous, "This is my son Ali".

The messenger bowed low.

"Salaam Aleikum", he said,

The youth smiled and made a gracious reply to the greeting, the Said looked on admiringly, then he spoke,

"In view of what you have told me, it is I think desirable, for my second son and perhaps two of my bodyguards to travel to England and join Tariq", he paused, the silence inviting some comment. The messenger nodded and murmured,

"I know him, truly a son to be proud of".

The Sheikh smiled and made a slight inclination of his head in acceptance of the flattery,

"I am proud, but, though fully confident of him being able to conduct himself with honour in the matter he is engaged in, I consider that Ai", he popped a hand on his son's shoulder, "should join Tariq at once".

"As you wish, but there is no need of guards, Prince Achmed has instructed me to go to England and help in resolving this situation, with your blessing of course."

The Sheikh smiled.

"So shall it be, you Ali mark Abdullah's words and inform Tariq that he must obey his wishes".

Karim shook his head,

"No exalted one, I go to serve your sons and shall only advise, not order."

The emissary bower again as he withdrew from the sheikh's presence.

Shortly afterwards, the palm trees bent again and the air filled with sand as the helicopter beat its way upwards, and like some ungainly flying insect seemed to waver slightly until the chopping rotor carried it up, up and further away until it disappeared in the sun's haze.

Sydney Bryant sat in his office at Whitley Warren mulling over the mysterious telephone call he had received from Sir Humphrey Wonnacott, when Peter Winfield tapped at the door and came in.
"Penny for them?"
"Eh?"
"Your thoughts Sid, penny for your thoughts".
"Oh I see, sit down Peter", he made a steeple of his fingers and placed the fingertips to his mouth, Winfield was about to comment again but Bryant began to speak.
"Sir Humphrey telephoned..."
Peter Winfield sat quietly as Sydney related the contents of the chairman's call.
"So," asked Winfield, "Is the plant opening again?"
Bryant was about to answer when the sound of a car horn made him rise from his seat and

cross to the window.

"Oh no", he peered towards the main entrance, "What the devil does that fool Gates think he's doing"?

"Picketing", Winfield commented, as Bryant continued,

"Go and tell that idiot to let that car pass, It's got to be the people from London".

"What the old man's on about?"

"I reckon so", Bryant said, "That's if the posh-looking car is the one I've seen at the Park Royal offices," He moved to the door, "come on Peter, I'll go with you".

As soon as the reluctant shop steward had been persuaded to let them through Emily parked the car in accordance with Doctor Bryant's waving arms and they got out.

"Sorry about that", said Bryant, "unions you know," he bustled around introducing himself, "Oh, and this is my chief assistant, peter Winfield, actually", he almost giggled, "He runs the place, I'm just a figurehead really!"

Dodging from one to the other, he shepherded them into the main building and up a short flight of stairs to his office.

"Sit down, sit down please, we'll have a drink, coffee, eh? Everyone like coffee?"

He switched on an electric kettle and busied himself with cups and an assortment of jars. "Shan't be long", he commented, "Got to do it like this, we've no facilities since we've been phased down, no workers," he shrugged, "So no canteen".

After further small talk, when they were settled with their drinks, Andrew took out the box containing the phial.

"If you're in charge here then you should have this," he offered it to Bryant.

"Not yet Mister, er, Craig, isn't it?"

"Yes," replied Andrew, "but you take it, I've got to contact Sir Humphrey Wonnacott to tell him that we've arrived, he told me to..."Bryant interrupted him.

"I recently had a phone call from our Lord and Master", Winfield made mock obeisance and Ben Acate, not knowing that it was meant sarcastically, followed suit and smiled benignedly, "Yes", continued Bryant, looking askance at the Arab's actions "Well Sir Humphrey has sent you down here with," he indicated the phial that Andrew still held, "but, as I told him, our chemists were made redundant more than a month ago".

Emily put down her coffee cup.

"Then why are we here?" she asked.

Bryant turned towards her,

"I don't rightly know to be honest; all I could grasp from the boss's conversation is that this potion could be the greatest thing since sliced bread, that's if we find out what it is!"

"But you're a chemist Doctor Bryant"?

"Not", the doctor squeezed the words out, Exactly Miss", he coughed, "you see dear lady, in reality I'm no more a chemist that you are, or are you?" he asked then smiled as she shook her head. "No well", they call me doctor purely as a courtesy title, Peter, mister Winfield, now he's a chemist, and no doubt if we ever get half the gear back that we had to get rid of from the laboratory over the past few months he'll be able to show you just how much of a chemist he is, right peter?"

"Oh yes, right you are," Winfield subsided into his seat, fully prepared to agree to anything, although he hadn't bothered to follow much of the conversation.

Andrew spoke,

"But you're in charge, if I give you this lotion we can go back to London yes?" he finished hopefully.

"No", replied Bryant, shaking his head, "the lotion", he tutted, "potion I mean, you've got it, and you keep it until sir Humphrey arrives".

"He's coming here?" Andrew asked incredulously.

Ben Acate nodded sagely,

"To bring my money no doubt".

Bryant looked at him, then at Andrew,

"Money?"

Andrew shot a hard glance at the Arab.

"That's all he's been on about since we set out, money and sex" he added scornfully.

"Nothing wrong with him then," said Winfield brightly, taking an interest in the proceedings now that his favourite subject had been mentioned, "Normal sort of bloke I would have thought", he winked at Ben Acate, "Spikka de English John?"

"Peter", Bryant said sharply, then to the Arab, "Forgive my friend, he's only joking. Aren't you?" he added pointedly to Winfield, as Peter nodded. Bryant continued to speak, "Anyway, now we've got to decide where we'll all sleep eh? Any preferences?"

Ben Acate stood and smiled at Emily,

"I will sleep with the lady", he pronounced,

"Oh no you won", stated Andrew, "See what I mean?" he asked.

"Take no notice Andrew", said Emily," He's only trying to annoy you", then to Bryant, "Is there a hotel in the village? And more important, is there any petty cash? We weren't prepared to stay".

"Ah, did I not tell you?" Bryant appeared sheepish, "Sir Humphrey said in his call that no one was allowed to leave, not until he arrives at least. So that means we sleep here, we've, er, we've got blankets and that, in fact we've got all kinds in our store haven't we Peter?"

"Have we?" Winfield was puzzled, then his face cleared, "Oh yes, all kinds we've got", he rose from his seat and beckoned to Bryant, "could I have a word?"

Doctor Bryant followed his assistant outside

the door of the office.

"What on earth is this about?" Winfield asked, "You never said anything about sleeping here and what about us? I certainly don't want to sleep in this bloody dump, I want to sleep in my own bed, and what about your wife? She won't like it is you tell her you're kipping in the factory, and as for bedding", he mimicked Bryant, "we've got blankets, oh yes, we've got all kinds in our stores, well you just tell me where…I…", Bryant interrupted him,

"Hold on we ran a night shift, they slept".

"Half of them were always asleep Sid, but not officially, we're just not geared up for anything like this".

"Well you soon will be, I'll see to that", the words, harsh, commanding, echoed up the corridor and made them both turn sharply, it was Sir Humphrey Wonnacott. He strode swiftly towards them, "all right then, where's Craig? Where's my potion".

Bryant, wordlessly, opened the door and he, together with Peter Winfield, trailed behind the chairman as he marched into the office.

Chapter 7

Tariq stood in the gallery at Gatwick airport and watched the private jet of Prince Achmed Yussuf, distinctive in its metallic blue and gold livery, touchdown and begin taxiing towards the main building. He waited until he saw a limousine sporting the same colours heading to the plane then made his way to the V.I.P. reception area.

His brother Ali, after being whisked through customs, spotted him immediately and embraced him, Tariq smiled.

"Ho, little brother, what news do you bring?" He punched Ali's upper arm playfully, "Why does our father, who is in all things wise, let his young child fly the skies alone"?

"Ha", snorted Ali, "I'm nearly twenty so make sure this child does not make you eat those words", then as Tariq grasped him in a bear-hug and squeezed, he gasped, "Enough Tariq, perhaps I shall make you eat your words another day", Tariq released him and Ali continued, "but I am not alone", he beckoned his uncle's aide forward, "This is Abdullah Karim. Remember? He will stay, guide and advise us".

Tariq stared for a moment, then remembering common courtesy, bowed.

"Salaam Alaikhum Karim, I know you, but...?" He looked mystified, "what guidance should I need? Surely the message reached my father..."?

"I can explain," Karim offered, but first, can we not leave this place and go to the hotel, I'm sure you both would like to eat and perhaps rest?"

"Hotel?" it was Ali's turn to be surprised, I had no idea you'd organised a hotel".

"I cannot take credit for planning", Abdullah smiled, "your uncle owns it, among other properties in London, and there is always room for his friends, and family", he stood aside and let the two brothers precede him from the lounge to where the limousine awaited them.

"Ah", said Tariq, "but I have a car", he pointed towards the decrepit, dark-coloured saloon that he had used to follow Ben Acate to Bradford, and back to Four-mile Services before it had let him down by breaking down. Karim looked at it and tutted.

"Dear me no, I'm sure we can find something better than that for you. The limousine, but no, perhaps something a little plainer, come, forget that", he sought for a word, "that er, vehicle, there are cars at the hotel, we can take one of those".

Tariq looked at him, then at the keys in his hand,

"But," he began. Ali took the keys from him and beckoned to a man standing nearby.

"Do you want a car?" He asked.

"Er, a car?" the man was puzzled, "what do you mean, how much like? Er…"

Ali thrust the keys into his hand and pointed at Tariq's car,

"Take that if you will".

The man glanced at it.

"Take it where?"

"Wherever you wish, "said Ali as he climbed into the back seat of the limousine with Tariq and Abdullah Karim, "It's yours".

As the gleaming monster eased silently away from the parking area, the man stood holding the keys and, as they reached the corner Ali looked back. Even from the distance he could see the bewilderment etched on the man's face. When they reached the hotel, Abdullah bustled about, arranging rooms, ordering meals, in English, then in French, again in Arabic, Tariq and Ali looked on , impressed by the efficiency of their uncle's representative.

Afterwards, they settled in the lounge where Abdullah ordered coffees.

"Now", he said leaning into the depths of an overstuffed armchair, "Obviously there are questions you would ask but..." he held up a hand for silence as Tariq attempted to speak "No, first hear my words and then ask what you will".

Tariq subsided and Karim continued.

"Your father, and his brother Prince Achmed, Yussuf, are as you know of royal blood, you are yourselves princes, but I digress, Prince Achmed who I have the honour to serve, followed the way of the merchant, the entrepreneur, your father trod the path as laid down by the prophet Ishmael, the way of the Bedouin, but he is of no less stature because of it, except your uncle is perhaps more worldly that your honoured father and it is perhaps this worldliness that tells him there is something afoot here. Ben Acate, we know from our agents, came to England and made several approaches to different people and now, we find that he has contacted Farm Chemicals Limited, and for what purpose, obviously to sell them the potion he has stolen from your father."

Tariq interrupted grimly,

"When I catch him it will be the last thing he ever will steal. He caused my father to lose face".

Abdullah smiled gently at him,

"There speaks a true son of his father, And Ali? Do you wish to strike down Ben Acate? To kill him? Or at least to chop off his hand so all men would know he is a thief?"

Ali looked from one to the other then, fixing his eyes on Karim, he spoke,

"It is the way is it not?" a thief must pay for his crime, it is written, but? he turned his head and raised a quizzical eyebrow,

"Kill him", growled Tariq

"Hush my bloodthirsty brother, something tells me our good friend Karim has other ways of skinning goats," Ali leaned forward.

Abdullah Karim shook his head,

"No", he said firmly, "I must make some telephone calls, and you two must sleep. Tomorrow you will know the plans your uncle and I have formulated. Tomorrow we find Ben Acate."

The next few hours illustrated just how Sir Humphrey had become Captain of the industry. The telephone became almost red-hot as he burnt up the lines with barked commands, phone-call after phone-call, builders, suppliers, and in between, the chairman's harsh orders to all and sundry. The small gathering listened and looked on in awe, then Peter Winfield spoke.

"Sir", he ventured, "why are we all sleeping in the factory?"

"I told them," Bryant offered, "I said you didn't

want anyone leaving, it's just a matter of bedding and..." his voice faded as the chairman snorted,

"Ha", he patted the box containing the potion that lay on his desk in front of him, "now I've got this you can sleep where you bloody well want to"; he turned to Andrew, "Craig, have you got anything against staying here for a few days?"

Andrew shook his head.

"Good, get down to the village and book a room at the hotel, the something Inn it's called, one for you, for Ben whassit there and er...,

He pointed the telephone receiver at Emily, Are you and him..." he raised a hand in silence as she made to answer,

"Hello", he said down the mouthpiece, "Yes, my manager will contact you tomorrow morning, no, I do not wish to speak to anyone else, I've told you. We need staff, you are the employment exchange, ergo, you supply staff. G
Good day to you", slamming the phone down he looked at Emily again "Well?" are you staying or what?"

"I'd like to sir", Emily's tone was uncharacteristically subdued, even she couldn't fail to be impressed by the efficient, though overbearing manner in which Sir Humphrey Wonnacott was directing operations.

"A Room for you then," once again the chairman dialled a number, then glared, "What are you waiting for?" Haven't I got through to you yet? You know what you're supposed to be doing? Get out, out!" his voice rose, "Go on the lot of you, Craig? He stopped Andrew as he went to leave, "Don't go anywhere tonight, I'll be down at that hotel to see you, go on now"; he waved a hand in dismissal as he turned his attention back to the telephone.

That evening, after they had settled into the hotel, Emily was speaking to Andrew in the lounge,

"If Sir Humphrey starts talking about what's happening here, try to pin him down to where we stand, chat to him about more money as well".

"Everything's paid for Emily, when I signed for the rooms the manager told me..."

"It might be", she broke in, "but what about your salary, and mine? What about spending money? Have you got anything left of that hundred quid?"

"Oh yes", Andrew put his hand in his pocket.

"No", said Emily sharply, "don't take it out here, that's yours".

"Take what out?" the peremptory bark of the chairman's voice was unmistakeable and they looked up.

"You aren't still at it are you?, Sir Humphrey leered, "with what I've seen up to now it's a wonder you've got anything left to take out".

"Sir", Emily crimsoned fiercely, and Andrew also blushed as he said,

"It's not very much sir, I had to give Ben Acate his return fare to Bradford, and there was the petrol..."

The chairman stared, started to ask a question and stopped, then said firmly,

"No, not again Craig, you confuse me enough as it is. Quiet now, I'll talk, you listen right? Andrew subsided.

"Of course sir, I was only..." his voice tailed away as the chairman fixed him with a flinty stare.

"Thank you", Sir Humphrey intoned. "Now," he sat down, "Drinks?"

Without waiting for an answer, he beckoned to Reg Anderson, who was hovering nearby,

"Three large brandies, he'll pay", indicating Andrew.

The drinks were bought and Emily, forestalling Andrew's attempt to get money from his [pocket, almost snatched the bill and crawled her name across it.

"Room number?" Reg asked.

She told him, then turning a defiant face to Sir Humphrey, stated

"On the firm sir, like you said."

"Did I?" the chairman sounded puzzled, then "Probably", he admitted, "anyway, I'm going to take you both into my confidence but , before I start, I asked if you would mind staying here for a few days, and I'll tell you why".

He paused to light a cigar, then told them of the take-over bid, the difficulties that Farm Chemicals faced at that moment, and also a

little of his own plans, "so you see" he puffed a cloud of smoke towards them as they hung attentively onto his words, "Next week it should be all over with, one way or another and either way, you'll both be well rewarded."
"Please", Ben Acate approached; "A reward sir?" is that my money you speak of?"
The chairman growled deep in his throat.
"Look Ben Nevis..."
"Ben Acate el...."
"Enough", sir Humphrey's face became mottled, "I don't want to hear all that bloody lot again, I've told you you'll get your money , God in Heaven man, aren't I doing enough for now? Same for these two, free room and board, expenses, drinks, all paid for out of my own pocket.
"The firm's pocket he means", Emily muttered.
"I heard that madam, I heard that", the chairman rose to his feet, his voice rose also and, almost shrieking, he said,
"You're like the rest of them, it's my firm, all mine, so the firm's pocket is my pocket right!" He made to stalk off, then suddenly turned, seemingly in control of himself again, "Here

young Craig, take this potion back, look after it until tomorrow or the day after, they should be ready at the plant by then, I've got to return to London, and remember, you're in charge of the whole shebang, I'm trusting you" as he turned away, he called back over his shoulder, "And go easy on those expenses, I'm not made of money you know".

That night, Andrew slept alone, or rather he stayed in his room alone, for he kept waking up and feeling desperately for the warmness of Emily that he had known, and now he missed...
The following day, Emily seemed to be avoiding any attempted discussion about their affair. Not that Andrew thought of it as that, no, to him it was pure, true, but at that moment unrequited love.
Ben Acate mooned around the inn, bending anyone's ear that cared to listen about his treatment by Sir Humphrey, wailing sorrowfully about the chairman's reluctance to pay him the money he considered was his

right.

Work at that plant continued, apparently from the various telephone messages received, non-stop, at the instigation of Sir Humphrey, whose absence didn't appear to lessen any threat of his wrath if his wishes were not fulfilled...

The second day, Andrew was sitting in the lounge, reading, when Emily say opposite,

She was silent for a moment, then

"I've been studying you".

"Oh yes", he tried to sound non-committal, but the familiar emotions when she was near sent hot blood coursing through his veins and caused his face to take on a pinkish hue,

"Why?" he asked.

She leaned forward and rested a hand on his knee,

"Sometimes you're so..." she sought for a word that would describe what she was trying to say, then , "Put it this way", her hand started a stroking motion, and Andrew's breath started to quicken

"Emily", trying to sound matter-of-fact, he could only emit a noise between a strangled cough and a wheezing entreaty, "Please, someone's watching, stop it"; he caught her hand and lifted it from his leg.

"Now that's what I'm trying to tell you "Emily said. "That's what's the matter with you, you're too stick-in-the-mud, too respectable, you don't let yourself go enough, look at you now".

Andrew stared at her instead, and then taking off his glasses asked plaintively

"What's the matter with me?"

She laughed, leaned forward and kissed him on the forehead.

"Nothing I suppose, still, let me see your spectacles a moment", he handed them over and was puzzled as Emily peered through the lens, "you might as well be looking through plain glass", she stated, "Why on earth do you wear them"?

Andrew flushed.

"Well, they were cheap", then he stared aghast, Emily's face grew crimson, she appeared to be choking,

"I say are you all right"? He half-rose from his seat, then subsided as her surpressed laughter came bubbling out.

"Cheap", she gurgled, "did you buy them

because they were cheap?"

"Of course not", he replied, "I wear them for reading", he added coyly, "anyway, they make me look distinguished, after all, I am an accountant".

Her mirth under control, Emily spoke,

"Yes you are, my little accountant, but honestly, you don't need your glasses to look distinguished, it's your manner that makes people sit up and take notice, that's why you've been picked for this job, Sir Humphrey must have been impressed with you, or be taking advantage of you," she added silently.

"Do you think so?" he gave a satisfied smile and sat straighter in his chair, then his expression changed, "Oh no, here comes that Arab, more moaning about his money I suppose".

"That's not Ben Acate", Emily observed, "It's a different Arab, and there's two more", they watched as Tariq and his brother Ali joined Abdullah Karim at the reception desk where they booked rooms.

"Are you staying long gentlemen?" asked Mrs Anderson, the lady who served as general dogsbody in the hotel, receiving guests, organising meals, anything and everything it appeared whilst, one presumed, being a wife to the genial host who seemed to spend all his time on the wrong side of the hotel bar.

"That depends", replied Abdullah, then bowed his thanks and led his companions into the lounge.

"Greetings", he inclined his head towards Andrew and Emily as Tariq and Ali sat nearby and smiled.

"I thought Arabs didn't drink?" Andrew muttered to Emily as they ordered coffee and liqueur brandies.

She shrugged then turned as Abdullah spoke, "Would it be disrespectful for me to offer you and your husband some refreshment?""That's very kind of you", Emily smiled acceptance as Andrew said, "I'm not her husband".

She stood and moved to the Arab's table, "Perhaps a coffee?" She sat down as Andrew said again, "I'm not her husband".

Abdullah waved away his explanation,

"A Brandy for you no doubt".

Andrew took the proffered glass as he sat

alongside Emily.

"Such a pleasant inn don't you think" Abdullah addressed his words to Ali, but he sought the eyes of Andrew as he spoke.

"It is nice," a brief remark, yet it seemed to exhaust Andrew's vocabulary and he sat studying his brandy glass.

Emily saw his disconcertment and volunteered her own contribution.

"We are only here for a while", she said, "we work for Farm Chemicals and Mister Craig here is in charge of their new project."

"How interesting", Abdullah smiled, "and what might this project be?"

It was then that Andrew became assertive, "Can't talk about it", he stated firmly, "Top secret it is, special orders from the chairman, Miss Lang is my assistant and we've got one of your countrymen helping us".

Tariq asked,

"An Arab you mean?"

As Emily nodded, Ali smiled at Abdullah and said,

"What a coincidence my friend, an Arab": then he turned to Emily, "there are many kinds of

Arab good lady, from many different countries, but..."

"Ben Acate's his name", blurted Andrew, then let his puzzled gaze meet that of Emily as the three men started to laugh...

"Did you get the impression that those Arabs knew Ben Acate"? Asked Andrew as he and Emily lay in her bed that night.

"Hush", Emily's tone was soft, muffled as she brushed her lips across his face, found his mouth with hers, then pressed her full length against him.

He shuddered, an ecstatic trembling that brought a sweat to his naked frame.

"I...I...Oh Emily, I only wondered..." the word died into an unintelligible mutter as he lost himself in what she was doing, his own hands and lips seeking to prolong this pleasurable torment.

Chapter 8

The following morning, Doctor Bryant and Winfield were with Ben Acate in the dining room of the Warren Inn, when Andrew virtually bounded into the room.

"Hello", he cried, a smile so wide on his lips that Winfield wondered whether in fact it went right round his head.

"Not eating?"

Andrew continued, striding over to their table and slapping Ben Acate on the back.

"Don't suppose they've got any sheep's eyes eh?" he guffawed, "Haw haw, never mind".

"You're in a good mood", commented Bryant, "Sleep well?"

Andrew beamed the thought of Emily and their night of passion fresh in his mind.

"Yes", he sighed, "A wonderful night thank you".

"Good", said the doctor, "Perhaps after breakfast you and your secretary could come to the plant with Ben Acate, everything's virtually complete now, the animal laboratory's stocked, your office is ready, and I'd like you to meet the staff we've took on. Seeing how Sir Humphrey left you in charge, I think it's only fitting that you should be there on our first day eh?"

"Of course", replied Andrew, thinking of what Doctor Bryant had said about his own office. He smiled self-satisfiedly, "I'll be glad to get rid of this at last"; he took the potion out of his pocket.

"Aiee", their eyes focussed on Ben Acate as he gabbled, "put it away, put it away".

As Andrew complied, Doctor Bryant shot an astounded look at the Arab.

"Mmm right then, we'll be on our way, coming Peter?"

"Surely my lord and master", Peter Winfield's tone was mocking, "Let us fly".

Ben Acate stood and cast a furtive glance around the room before saying,

"I too must leave", he grasped Bryant's arm, "At once! Can I accompany you?"

"Well, I, er, of course you can, er what about

you Mister Craig? Do you have a car"?

"I think so", Andrew replied, "Emily's the driver, but he turned to the Arab, "Don't you want to wait and come up with us?

There's three of your countrymen here, booked in last night, and they know you, at least they smiled when they heard your name."

Ben Acate didn't smile, he didn't even essay a slight grin, in fact, he looked positively sick and spoke urgently to Doctor Bryant,

"Can we go now? Please. Can we go?"

"Yes", answered Bryant, then to Andrew, "We'll see you later then", his words fell on deaf ears. Emily had entered the room and was walking towards them.

"Come on, " Peter Winfield tugged at Bryant's sleeve, then nodded at Andrew and Emily as they gazed into each other's eyes, "Can't you see we're intruding"?

"Oops", smiled Bryant, and waved a farewell to the unheeding couple as he led the way from the dining room.

"They've gone", whispered Emily.

"Yes", he replied, taking her hand.

"Shouldn't we go as well"?

"Mm-mm", Andrew murmured

"If that means no", said Emily, "then I'm quite willing to stay here, but what if Sir Humphrey comes?"

"Let him", said Andrew bravely, still lost in her presence, then as the implication of what she had said sunk in, he dropped her hand, "What if he does come back though, we'd better go eh?"

Emily chuckled.

"I thought you might change your mind, I'll get the car".

At the plant, Andrew and Emily got out of the car and stood for a long moment, staring at each other before being interrupted by Peter Winfield.

"Hey you two", he said briskly, "Old Bryant's sent me out to see if you two are coming in or staying here to take root".

"What?" Andrew asked, then, as realisation dawned, "Yes, we're coming in".

Hand in hand, he and Emily followed Winfield

as he led them inside the building and along the ground floor corridor to a small room.

"There!" he announced, throwing open the door and standing back for them to enter, "Welcome to your new office, actually, most of it is new". He stepped inside and pointed to the desk, "That was here before, but the posh chair, that was specially bought by your mate the chairman, get it?"

"Chair, chairman?" noticing their blank looks he shook his head, "Never mind", he said, "the rest of the clan is waiting for their new boss-man, down the passage here, second door on the right", he made to leave but Andrew stopped him.

"We'll go with you", he took out the potion, "I've got to hand this over haven't I"?

"Dunno", said Winfield, "I'm just one of the peasants round here. Mind you, it'll probably be me who's got to look at it so bring it along by all means. Let's have a sniff", he took it from Andrew and opened the top, "Not much of a pong is it?" Andrew leaned forward to smell and Winfield tipped the bottle at the same time.

"No", Andrew's voice was panic-stricken, "you've spilled it, what will sir Humphrey say?" He hastily brushed a hand over his trousers and looked askance at the splashes of liquid on the floor.

Invisible, pervasive, the aroma wafted along the corridor, spreading it's seemingly innocuous tendrils into every corner of the building.
In the laboratory, Miss Allen, the assistant who had been employed to look after the animals, gazed vacantly at the activity as the aroma filtered into the lab and made the animals restless, then, as she got a whiff of the potion herself, smiled knowingly and, humming softly, walked along the front of the cages, freeing the occupants as she went.
The only canine tenant, a non-descript mongrel of some unknown extraction, barked, leapt excitedly to the floor and bounded out of the laboratory. Padding softly along the passage-way, the animal paused at the slightly open door that led to where Andrew was

meeting the staff, growled deep in it's throat, then entered and made a bee-line for the source of the aroma, Andrew's trousers! Andrew Craig was non-plussed, he tried to concentrate on the face of the man who was speaking to him, but all the time was aware of the other people in the room acting rather strangely. Of course he realised that friendliness was by far the best approach when it came to introducing oneself for the first time in any job, but kissing? And what were the couple in the corner doing? The man he was addressing excused himself as a young woman pulled him away gently and Andrew looked for someone else to talk to, then became conscious of the dog. It sniffed vigorously at his trousers, Andrew shook his leg, and moved off, the dog pounced again, snuffled, then took a mouthful of the material in it's jaws, Andrew lifted his leg, bringing the dog with it, and stared helplessly about him, his face growing red, "Get off", he cried "Go away".

Other people, their attention drawn from their own involvements, began to take an interest in what was happening.

Someone giggled and, as Andrew started for the door, hopping on one leg, then dragging the firmly attached dog with the other, hysterical laughter exploded all around him and shattered what little poise he had left.

He almost screamed with frustration as he staggered through the door then closed it quickly behind him and turned to see his secretary staring at him.

"Please…" it was a heartfelt entreaty, "Get it off me", he beseeched her in a voice so tremulous she expected to see tears forming in his eyes. Emily bent down, and as she grabbed the cur by the scruff of the neck to drag it from it's new-found soul-mate, there was a ripping noise as a strip of Andrew's trouser leg remained in the dog's teeth and flapped as she sent the animal on it's way with a firm kick to it's rear end.

"Th…thank you", Andrew stuttered. He took a deep inhalation of his asthma spray, "You saved me, that was embarrassing, most embarrassing indeed, but the people," he indicated the door behind him,

"They're, they're"

Smiling she said, "Andrew the dog's gone".
He shook his head wildly.
"No, you don't understand the people in there". Emily wondered what he was on about, then her own nostrils twitched, and she felt an overpowering urge to touch him, caress him. Involuntarily she moved closer, her heart pounding and her full lips trembling. A shuddering sigh shook her frame as her eyes closed and she reached out for him.
"Yes," said Andrew, "Well, I'll er, I better see about changing these trousers, I'll see you later".
Eluding her clutching hands, he almost scuttled back along the corridor.
Emily stifled an urge to follow as she stared at his receding back, then thought to herself, 'what was wrong with him'? but more important, 'What was wrong with her?'
Back in his office, Andrew sniffed deeply at the air.
"It's the potion", he muttered, "Stinking the place out". He sat behind his desk, "Yes" then he stood up again, "It must be stopped, if it carries on we'll have to evacuate the building".

For a moment he was at a loss, whatever could he do? Then inspiration, he would tell Bryant. Going into the corridor, he moved to the door he thought he's come from and opened it. It was a laboratory of some sort. A bench was lined with retorts and, as he stepped inside he saw that they were each over their own Bunsen burner, lit, that made the glassware bubble away like some scene from a horror movie. A witch's cauldron effect with different coloured streams of vapour emerging from the necks of every flask.

Moving closer, he studied the layout then listened intently as he heard a noise. Strange, it didn't appear to be coming from the equipment, yet it was, wasn't it?

He bent forward and peered over the bench then leapt back swiftly, consternation on his face. It was a woman, and, yes, Ben Acate. The moaning noise emanated from the parted lips of Miss Allen, the laboratory assistant, who lay sprawled under the weight of the Arab as he moved purposely on top of her.

Andrew's visage resembled that of a ripe plum as he sped from the scene and made for the comparative isolation of his own office once again.

Calling frantically for Emily, he picked up the telephone and dialled London; Sir Humphrey had to be told.

While waiting for the connection he called out again but there was no reply, either from the phone or his errant secretary.

corridor. Pacing past the half-open doors of the lab and other rooms, he couldn't help but notice that the aroma was getting stronger; his own breathing was becoming heavier so he took out his inhaler and used it. Suddenly a squealing sound made him limp quickly along to another door next to the laboratory, he entered. It was the room where the animal cages were, He stared in amazement...Hamsters, rabbits, mice, and guinea pigs, they had all been released and were vigorously copulating in every corner of the room.

"Oh no", groaned Andrew.

Chapter 9

Abdullah Karim was using the hotel telephone when Tariq and Ali emerged from the dining room and waited for him to finish.

"Have you eaten?" asked Ali as Karim replaced the receiver.

"Yes", replied Abdullah, "but let us have coffee, I am returning to London and we must talk before I go".

When they were settled in the lounge, the two brothers gave their attention to what Karim had to tell them, then, when he paused to have a drink, Tariq asked,

"But what of us? Are we to come to London? And what of Ben Acate? Does he remain unpunished"?

"Patience brother", Ali chided, "Be guided by Karim, has he not brought us here when we did not know where to look for Ben Acate?" he turned to his uncle's mentor, "Tariq grows impatient, he has no stomach for the machinations of intrigue, he would much rather go to this factory place, take the potion, and then separate Ben Acate from whatever part of his anatomy that come closest to the blade of his knife".

Tariq's eyes glinted as he nodded willingness to follow such a course of action but Karim held up both of his hands in mock horror.

"Allah forbid", he said, "that is not the way of the western world, imagine", he tutted, "the English policemen finding bits of Ben Acate scattered all over their beautiful countryside, no, he will suffer", Karim's tone fell to a sepulchral whisper, "But he will suffer in a longer, more lasting fashion" he laughed.

"Ha, I'm sounding as bloodthirsty as you Tariq, but enough, I will leave the car and, if you wish, go to this factory, see what is happening there, but do nothing, and when I return I promise you, you will understand more of the scheme we are embarked on. Now here are the keys", he looked at Ali who shook his head and indicated Tariq.

"there is my driver; he has much experience of the English roads".

"for just a few days." Tariq commented, "still perhaps an older head is better for anything, including driving," he accepted the proffered keys as Abdullah stood.

"Salaam Aleikhum"

"Aleikhum us Salaam", the brothers rose as one and made obeisance as Abdullah Karim swept from the room.

Sir Humphrey sat at his desk and scarcely moved, his secretary placed a memo in front of him,

"The board meeting", she said, and tossed her head coquettishly before leaving the room.

The chairman wasn't impressed by such antics however; his glum face reflected the blackness of his thoughts. He stabbed broad finger at the desk intercom.

"Sir"? Lorraine's voice, questioning, came booming from the loudspeaker, and Sir Humphrey hastily turned the volume down.

"Bloody oath", he exclaimed

"Sir?" there was puzzlement in the girl's tone

"nothing, nothing", he said resignedly, then

"Hold on though, ask Tom Allenby to pop round and see me".

"He won't be able to right away Sir Humphrey; he has a gentleman with him".

"I see", the chairman thought for a moment, "how the devil do you know that Lorraine? You're my secretary not Allenby's".

"But sir", he imagined her hurt expression, "I saw the man when I dropped in the memo about the board meeting, yours is on the desk, I..."

"Yes, yes", he interrupted, "Let me know when he's free eh? He switched off the intercom. Suddenly he picked up the telephone and dialled the code for Whitley Warren, then the number of the factory,

'Ring-ring', his finger tapped on the desk in time with the noise, 'Ring-ring' impatiently he slammed the phone down and pushed the intercom again,

"Sir?" Lorraine, ever-vigilant, answered.

"Whitley Warren", sir Humphrey barked, "there's no answer from the factory, get me a connection as soon as possible," he paused, "And that pub come hotel in the village, don't know what it's called, get the number of that while you're at it, and I still want to see Allenby", he didn't wait for a reply, just switched off and sat thinking.

After a few minutes Lorraine interrupted his reverie as she entered,

"The hotel sir, I've got through, a Mister Anderson?" she pointed to his telephone as Sir Humphrey swung to face her.

"Anderson? Who the hell is Anderson"?

"The proprietor I believe," Lorraine was used to the chairman's brusque attitude but she still felt resentment whenever he acted like this, "you did say you wanted to talk to the hotel" Sir Humphrey picked up the receiver and waved a hand of dismissal.

"I wanted the bloody number girl, but it doesn't matter. Hello." He snapped "Let me speak to Craig", he listened a moment, "Put the Arab on then, I'll speak to him".

He cupped the receiver in his hand and looked to where Lorraine stood, "All right, you can go," then he noticed her face, "and don't look so bloody miserable, I'm sorry I spoke harshly, but believe me, I've got a hell of a lot on my

mind, go on now, go and do some work, oh, and don't forget Mister Allenby please".
The secretary's face showed more than a touch of amazement as she heard his apology, the chairman saying sorry? She stepped out and closed the door carefully behind her; this would make some story for the coffee break.

At Whitley Warren, Anderson, the hotel owner, was standing by the reception desk; he's asked Sir Humphrey to wait while he fetched the Arab, but which Arab? He wished his wife was there, she arranged the bookings, she knew who was in the hotel. The Tariq and Ali walked Through the small lobby and Anderson's face brightened, two Arabs. He stepped forward.
"would one of you speak to sir Humphrey Wonnacott please?"
Ali smiled.
"It is the custom?"
"He's like to speak to an Arab, it's sir Humphrey, the chief of that fertiliser place up the road!" Anderson was becoming impatient, "Here, take the phone, I've got things to do", he

walked away as Ali picked up the receiver.

"Salaam, is this sir, I am talking to?"

"what the hell is going on?" the chairman's loud tone reverberated down the wires, "what developments are there"?

"Lots, I should think, it is a pleasant area", Ali's tone was matter-of-fact.

Sir Humphrey held the receiver away from his ear and glared at it, pleasant indeed.

"Now look", he snarled, "you're not bloody well down there to enjoy yourself, no matter what kind area it is. Has Craig gone to the factory? And if he has, why haven't you gone with him?"

"Ah", commented Ali, "Mister Craig?"

"Mister Craig", Sir Humphrey repeated bitingly. "Very nice man, I had coffee with him and his good lady last night, It is true, he left this morning, I think to..."

"I know where he was going", the chairman screamed, "what I want to know is why you're not with him. What are you doing now?"

"Talking to you, good sir". Ali was the very model of politeness.

"Stop", groaned Sir Humphrey, "I can't take

any more. Look go to the factory and get Craig to ring me, in fact, Ben whatever your name is, get anyone to ring me, I must know what's going on".

Carefully replacing the receiver, he sat, head in hands, and uttered a silent prayer to help him through this traumatic day.

Ali stared reflectively at his handset then, putting it on it's rest, said,

"I think that the sir who was speaking is the man who has our potion, He's told me to go to the factory because he is under the impression that I am Ben Acate."

"are you sure?" he asked his brother, "could it be that your English is not good enough to understand?"

"Ha", exclaimed Ali, "even your slight command of this alien tongue would not mistake what was said. Abdullah suggested we might visit this factory place, and now we've been ordered to do that very thing". He smiled, "come Tariq, your horsemanship is without question superb, now show me how you can drive a car. Take us to this factory, let us find again Ben Acate and maybe we will recover what is rightfully ours."

Chapter 10

Eddy Gates hovered around the entrance to the Farm Chemicals processing plant feeling like a fish out of water. For the last couple of days he had diligently stood in the roadway outside the gate and spoken to many drivers who had made deliveries, but to no avail. Not one of them had observed the single-handed picket he had set up and , quite frankly, although somewhere inside him was the thought that he was a knight in shining armour doing battle for what was right, after much soul-searching, he was coming round to the idea that he was behaving exactly as someone had described him, a proper prat! He'd watched all kinds of gear being brought into the factory, the teams of builders who had worked day and night to effect the transformation in the main office block, he'd even seen new the new faces that had been engaged and he still felt as if he didn't exist, things just carried on around him. Thinking he would have a few words with the convenor, Fred Alexander, he started walking towards the office when a woman emerged from the doorway and waved. Eddy returned the greeting, then gasped,

"My God, she's naked".

"Yoo-hoo", she cried, and made a gesture that was an unmistakeable invitation.

Gates broke into a staggering run towards her, "Blimey", he muttered, "Cor Blimey".

Then a car horn sounded and he stopped. A large car had pulled up at the gates and what looked like an Arab had got out and was shouting at him.

"Excuse me", it was Ali, his headdress blowing about his face, "come here please".

"No", Eddy mouthed the word desperately, "No, I can't, not now", he looked towards the woman who smiled and struck a provocative pose before turning away and indicating that he should follow.

Turning again, Eddy croaked hoarsely, 'please wait, er, love, whoever you are, hang on a minute' then he uttered a heart-felt moan of disappointment as a man appeared, picked her up in both arms and gave a triumphant shout as he carried her into the office building.

"Bastard", exclaimed Eddy feelingly.

"Pardon"? Ali had approached and was at Eddy's side.

"Er," Gates was non-plussed, "no not you, I, er.."

Ali interrupted.

"It is permitted to drive within the gates?"

"Sorry", said Eddy, his mind still on what might have happened between the man and the woman and what might have happened to himself in the man's place before this foreigner turned up and spoilt his chances. He sighed "What was that?"

Ali stared and remained polite as he said, "We have been sent by your, Sir Humphrey is it? And if you are the keeper of the gate then I ask if it is permitted to drive within the portal or.."

"Sir Humphrey Wonnacott?" Gates was impressed, "Of course, of course you can come in", he started towards the entrance and Ali walked alongside, "It's not locked you know, and I'm not the gatekeeper, but I'll open them for you". He pointed to where Emily had parked the firm's limousine, "you can put your car over there."

Tariq drove in and parked as Gates walked over with Ali.

"Do you want to see anyone special?" he asked as Tariq got out of the car, "Doctor Bryant's in charge or there's another boss, A Mister Craig, and one of your lot, I mean an Arab, like what you are".

"Do not trouble yourself on our account," said Ali patiently, "we shall go and see if anyone can help us".

"That's what I mean", said Eddy Gates, "You can't go walking round on your own, I'll take you to see Bryant, ok?"

"As you wish", said Ali, and together with Tariq, he followed Gates into the building.

Hearing footsteps, Andrew backed towards the half-open door and sidled through, pulling it closed behind him, he looked appealingly at Eddy Gates and the two Arabs he had spoken to last night.

"Something's wrong", he gurgled, "Everyone's gone sex-mad, what can I do?"

Ali sniffed the air.

"The potion"!

Tariq growled an agreement, then added, "It is very strong little brother, we must do something. You!"

Gates visibly jumped as Tariq jabbed a finger at his stomach, "Get water, lots of water!"

"What for?" asked Gates, not at all sure he should be taking orders. He needn't have bothered though, Tariq had spotted a fire-hose and was busily unreeling it.

"The potion", Ali said, for the first time showing impatience, "We must dilute it, weaken it's power".

"Power", Andrew sounded incredulous, "do you mean that stuff Mister Winfield is testing, what he spilled over my trousers, that's got something to do with this?" He opened the door into the laboratory and shuddered as he saw the animals were still as he had left them.

"Mister Craig, sir", said Ali gravely as he glanced over Andrew's shoulder, "it has everything to do with this".

"Oh my gawd", Eddy Gates stared past the two of them, "They're all at it", he said, "Having a .."

"We can see what they're having", said Andrew sharply, "so keep your comments to yourself".

"All right", Eddy countered, then caught a whiff of the aroma that emanated from Andrew's trousers, "Smells a bit don't it?"

"One ceases to notice it after a while", said Ali in Arabic, then in English, "you find it attractive?" he laid a hand gently on Eddy's cheek "The perfume is stimulating".

"Eh you, get off, stop that", Eddy leapt back into the corridor and Tariq, who had seen the effect the aroma was having on his brother came up fast with the hose.

"It is strong here", he announced.

"My trousers", said Andrew, It was spilt on my.." his words were lost in a violent gush of water as Tariq put the hose on full jet and directed it at his midriff, "Oof", he uttered as he was sent tumbling and skidding up the corridor.

"Open the windows", ordered Tariq, "Ali, go

outside in the fresh air. I will dilute the potion", he turned the nozzle to spray and, as Eddy moved quickly to the window, he too was soaked as Tariq entered the room with the hose going full blast.

The animals, squealing and creaming, were swept into a bedraggled mass of sodden fur. Then just as quickly separated to float hither and thither on the tidal wave created by Tariq and the fire-hose.

In the passage-way, Andrew got to his feet and staggered back to the doorway.

"What?"

Tariq turned and once again Andrew caught the full force of the water which sent him reeling back against the opposite wall gasping for breath.

The Arab spun round and Eddy Gates, thoroughly saturated, sought escape by diving through the open window. He landed at the feet of Ali who was breathing deeply, trying to rid himself of the effects of the potion. He leaned down to help Eddy.

"No you don't", Gates said, scrambling to his feet, "Stay away from me", he backed off several paces, then turning, squelched around the corner of the building.

Inside the corridor was rapidly filling with people, some in various stages of undress, almost trance-like in their movements as they milled about aimlessly. Voices were raised in query and Tariq, hearing them, emerged from the laboratory, still carrying the hose, and proceeded to damp down everybody in range of the spray.

The Ensuing screams and entreaties to "Turn the bloody thing off", caused Tariq to fiddle with the nozzle, twist it to full jet and inadvertently direct it along the corridor where it caught the mass of people who jumped all ways to evade it. One unfortunate put his elbow into the break-glass fire alarm point and the cacophony of noise was complimented by the clamour of alarm bells.

"Fire", someone shouted, the cry was taken up by others and, panic stricken, the crowd began to paddle their way through the flood that eddied and swirled in the shambles of the passage-way.

Andrew Craig, head throbbing with the start if

a migraine and absolutely soaked through, decided that enough was enough.

Deep within him some spark ignited and he stood, eyes flashing and screamed in a manner that would not have been amiss on a parade ground,

"Quiet, everybody quiet now".

He took two stiff-legged paces towards Tariq, "switch off that infernal hose-pipe", he hissed threateningly, and then he turned to the others, "Everybody outside, no running, walk, quietly, I want this building cleared until we can sort out this mess. Where's Doctor Bryant?"

Someone volunteered the information that he had been seen going into his office.

Emily Lang, disentangling herself from the embrace of a young man who was staring in some embarrassment at her as he came round from the influence of the aroma, was amazed at the masterful attitude showed by Andrew, She walked over to him.

"Andrew", she said softly.

"Not now Emily if you don't mind, please help me to clear these people from the corridor, get them outside".

"Yes", Tariq spoke, "the air is the best cure". Andrew looked at him, "who the devil are you anyway?" he asked, "Do you want Ben Acute?"

"Eventually" purred Tariq, "Eventually".

"What are you doing here?" Andrew persisted.

"My brother and I were ordered here by your Sir Humphrey, I carry a message. He would like to speak to someone, anyone".

"And I'd like to speak to him", said Andrew firmly as he stalked off in search of the missing Doctor Bryant.

Chapter 11

Without any cleaners being employed, an unimaginable oversight by Sir Humphrey, it was decided that everyone should concentrate on the ground floor and put right the shambles that had ensued from the effects of the aroma and the thousands of watery gallons bestowed on the building by the well meaning Tariq. Several of the more haughty members of the staff were reluctant to join in this 'Operation Mop-up', but, on being reminded of their behaviour whilst under the influence of the potion, they set to work with gusto.

Ben Acate had disappeared. After being in the laboratory with Miss Allen, he had come into the corridor where Tariq was plying the fire hose, caught a soaking that brought him rapidly from his semi-trance, then recognising who had drenched him, didn't stay to remonstrate, but left the building at speed. Eddy Gates had discovered the name of the naked woman who had waved at him and licked his lips as a salacious thought sped across his mind. Then he shuddered with frustration for nothing had happened, at least with him nothing had happened and Eddy wanted to put things right in that respect, he'd telephoned and she'd agreed to meet him at the hotel.

Pushing a mop along the downstairs corridor, he came to the staircase, then made his way furtively to Bryant's office. Holding his ear to the door he could hear the doctor talking to Winfield so, leaving the mop against the wall, he ran downstairs again and slipped curiously into the laboratory that adjoined the animal quarters.

"Anyone there?" he called, not expecting a reply, He moved slowly round the room examining the various items on the benches.

"Gotcher"!

Gates spun round as the voice of Peter Winfield sounded in his ears.

"Don't panic", Winfield slapped him on the shoulder, "It's only me, picketing the lab now?"

"No, I , er, don't be daft", Eddy found the

breath to answer him, "I was just looking , that stuff, it got everybody going didn't it?"

Winfield grinned hugely.

"Didn't it just, and it was only a spoonful or so".

"Is, er, is it, well, have you got any left?"Asked Eddy casually, "or has Craig took it?"

"What do you want it for , got something in mind?"

"Not really", answered Eddy, "I just wondered".

Winfield gazed quizzically at Gates.

"I don't know", he stated, "You're a bit of a dark horse on the quiet, anyway, Craig hasn't got it, he's gone back to the village with his secretary", he pointed to a small bottle that stood on top of one of the sink units, "And that's what's left, that little drop there".

"Oh", commented Eddy, "Well it's not important, see you later", he left the laboratory and Peter Winfield, smiling went through the door into the animal quarters.

"Shush", he said to Miss Allen, who was re-caging some hamsters.

"I beg your pardon?" she said.

Winfield held a finger to his lips, "Don't speak",

he whispered, then beckoned her to join him where he stood peeping into the other laboratory. She crossed the room and together they watched as Eddy Gates slipped into the lab, picked up the phial of liquid and crept out again.

"He's stolen something", she said, "Your chemicals!" then stared askance as Winfield started to laugh,

"It's water", he gurgled, "Tap water, He asked me about the potion and I told him that was it there, Water!" he wagged a finger, "don't tell him".

"Why should I tell him", she asked, "I've got more to worry about than your childish games with Mister Gates, there's still a lot of hamsters missing!"

Peter Winfield choked on a fresh outburst of laughter.

"What's wrong now?" she enquired testily.

"Nothing love, honestly, but hamsters? With what they were doing in here it shouldn't be long before you've got an abundance of the little ..."

"Mister Winfield", she stopped him, "I.. Then

colouring as she remembered that she herself had been under the influence of the potion, "I think you're disgusting". She sped from the scene leaving a puzzled Peter Winfield saying to himself,

"What did I say?"

Agatha Manners sat in the lounge of the Warren Inn sipping delicately at a gin and tonic.

Dressed in a sober two-piece suit and a spotless white blouse, she bore little resemblance to the uninhibited creature that showed such brazenness in flaunting her nudity whilst under the effect of the aroma. She wondered whether she was doing the right thing in agreeing to meet Eddy Gates, after all. It must have been embarrassing for him. Still, she must make every effort to apologise for her wanton behaviour.

Eddy Gates came in and glanced around the room two or three times before he identified Agatha as the woman he had come to meet. He walked over.

"It is you then?"

"Yes", she answered shyly.

He sat down then stood up again,

"Sorry, would you like a drink?"

"In a moment", Agatha was sure now, she shouldn't have agreed to this meeting, shouldn't have spoken to this man.

Eddy sat down and eyed her speculatively, "And you said er, you're not married?"

"Divorced", her answer almost lost in the hum of conversation that went on around them.

"Sorry!" Eddy smiled, feeling that this was surely to be his night.

"Divorced" louder now, then nervously expansive, "No children, he said my work wouldn't allow it, our work that is, he was always going on about our roles, our relationships, I..." she stopped.

"What a shame", commented Eddy, "I can see you as a mother, you look the type", he felt in his pocket for the bottle he had brought.

Agatha drained her glass and struggled to catch her breath as the liquor went down the wrong way. Her face reddened and she croaked hoarsely,

"Please, another gin and tonic".

Eddy took the proffered glass then patted her back and waited for her colour to return to normal before going to the bar and bringing drinks back for them both.

"Thank you", she said as he made himself comfortable beside her. He smiled and lifted his glass in a silent toast.

Agatha moved along the seat.

"I must go in a moment".

"But it's early Mrs, or can I call you Agatha", he placed his glass on the table and continued, "You know I was sorry I couldn't come to you when you were asking, when you…"

"When what?" Agatha asked in surprise.

"When you was, well", his eyes fell and he mumbled, "When you had nothing on".

Agatha blushed then said firmly, "you mustn't take notice of that, there were quite a few people acting out of character while that dreadful smell existed".

Eddy felt again for the phial he had stolen from Winfield's laboratory. Taking it out, he uncorked the bottle and waved it gently in front of Mrs Manner's face,

"You mean it was the potion that made you want me?"

She coloured even more but her tone was icy and she said, "I didn't, as you put it, want you, and what are you doing?"

"Nothing", grinned Eddy, placing a finger half over the neck of the bottle and sprinkling some drops of water onto her pristine white blouse, "It gets you doesn't it?"

Agatha's visage hardened,

"Do you mind?" she asked in a small tight voice, "That's a new blouse you're wetting".

Eddy wondered frantically when the stuff was going to work. Some people nearby were taking an interest in what he was doing, but ignoring them, he dribbled some liquid onto his fingers and flicked the drops directly into Agatha's face.

"You could want me again, couldn't you?" he suggested.

She stood up and wiped her face with the sleeve of her jacket and cried sharply,

"Stop it".

Eddy rose also and flicked more water at her, now he was puzzled, why wasn't it working?

"Feel it", he cried desperately, "Is it getting to you?"

"I said stop it", she screamed, causing everybody in the room to fix their attention on them.

Reg Anderson popped his head in from the bar and was amazed to see Agatha Manners striding angrily towards the exit pursued by a bemused Eddy Gates who was spraying her with liquid from a small bottle and crying, "Smell it baby, smell it!"

Slack-jawed, Anderson turned back to the bar and called for a large whiskey.

"What was the fuss, "asked his wife as she served him. He took a swallow of his drink, "D'ye know," he said slowly, "I just couldn't begin to explain".

Sir Humphrey's private telephone buzzed and he studied it for quite some time before picking up the receiver.

"Hello", he said meekly.

"Who's that?" came the question, "Humphrey?" The chairman nodded, then, realising the inanity of his action, snapped a reply in his old brusque manner.

"Of course it's me, who would you expect on my private line?"

"That's you alright", Tom Allenby chuckled, "Are you busy, can I bring someone in for you to meet"?

"Am I busy?" listen Tom, "I've been trying to get hold of you for the past half hour or so, it's you who's supposed to be have been busy".

"And so I was", Allenby said, "come on now; don't get uptight at this stage of the game, why, in no time at all it should all be finalised."

"Don't tell me that Tom, you've already tried to put the wind up me by saying that I could be thrown out with nothing. From my own firm mind you, the firm I built up with my bare hands, the firm I ..."

"You bought it!" Allenby interrupted.

"All right, built the bloody thing up after I bought it, it's still mine, and who are you to tell me anyway? You were nothing and I've done everything for you, yes, and made you Managing Director".

"Well, I wouldn't exactly say I was nothing, but

as for the M.D., yes, I knew that was you, and I'm grateful, but why the sudden outburst?" Tom Allenby sounded perplexed, "What's happened?"

"Nothing's happened", screamed the chairman, "That's what's wrong, I'm stuck here, all these plans you're making I don't know anything about, and what you've told me isn't worth a damn. What are you trying to do to me?"

"Calm down Humphrey", said Tom Allenby firmly, "I'm coming in".

The click of the receiver sounded in the chairman's ear and he paused in his tirade, listened for a moment, and then dropped his own handset onto its rest.

He looked up as Tom Allenby entered.

"You hung up on me", he said petulantly, "While I was speaking, cut me off".

"But I was coming in", Allenby was surprised, "You think I did it on purpose? Good lord, I was worried about you, something seems to be getting you down".

"Ha-ha", the chairman gave a desultory laugh, "Getting me down eh? Something is getting me down and I'm rapidly coming round to the idea that that something is you?"

"Me?" Allenby sounded incredulous, he sat heavily in the chair facing Sir Humphrey's desk, "you stagger me, you certainly do and ..."

"listen" the chairman interrupted him, "I took you from the salesman, made you senior sales executive, nursed you, then got you on board as a Sales Director, and last year, " he paused dramatically, "Managing Director".

He pointed an accusing finger, "I fought to have you in that position, my managing director, and I bet you've got more shares in this company that I have, the way you've been performing, stabbing me in the back whenever you could ..."

Tom Allenby leaned forward, white-faced and in a voice trembling with emotion said,

"You've got the gall to say I've been stabbing you in the back? Why you stupid bigot, you've been living off my back lately, I tell you straight, if it wasn't for me and some members of the board the receivers would have been in by now. You swan around in your flash car, the firm's car actually, you smoke those foul cigars", tom stood up, "left to you you'd be rolling your own cigarettes and catching buses, I told you, once you didn't pick up those shares you let go, and the firm started to decline, that was the writing on the wall , it was...Oh why the hell should I bother, I should just let you, and your bloody firm sink", he turned away then swung round to face Sir Humphrey, "and seeing you're surmising, yes I do have more shares in the company that you, but it's no good having shares in a company that's going down so fast it'll finish up in Australia or somewhere". He pointed at the door, "I wanted you to meet a man who could possibly save you, or save something out of the wreckage if we went down, but what's the use? I got you Ben Acate in the first place and you haven't bothered!"

"I have, I have", Sir Humphrey jumped to his feet, "I got it organised at Whitley Warren; personally, you know I did, I can't help it if you arranged a board meeting".

"The board arranged it's own meeting;" said Tom, "but where's the results from Whitley Warren? It doesn't take forever to analyse a liquid does it?"

"That's not my doing ", said the chairman defensively, "I'm waiting for someone to contact me".

"Well", Tom sounded reluctant, though his manner had mellowed. He came to the desk and sat down again, "What about this chap then, want to hear what he's got to say?"

Sir Humphrey lowered himself into his own chair,

"I'm in your hands Tom what is he suggesting?"

"Money Humphrey, an immediate injection of capital that should strengthen our position and shut out any other interested parties".

Sir Humphrey's brain started to tick over a little faster. Money he could understand, his face relaxed.

"And what's in this for the money man?" he couldn't resist this jibe, "does he wasn't more shares than me as well as the office cat?"

"Touché", Tom grinned, "Not exactly that. No matter which way it goes though, I can't see you remaining at the helm. Still, retirement from a flourishing company? Golden handshake de-luxe I should think!"

"He wants me out?"

"Not in so many words Humphrey, but he's on about a new name for the company and refurbishment of this building so they can still have a London headquarters."

"More lies Tom?" asked the chairman, "you told me this building was rented".

Tom nodded.

"It is Humphrey, this chappie represents the owners, the people we pay our rent to, ready?" He crossed to the door.

Sir Humphrey waved a hand, "Wheel him in", he said.

"Come in please", Tom Allenby ushered in the visitor, "This is Sir Humphrey Wonnacott, Sir Humphrey, allow me to present..."

"Salaam," said Abdullah Karim, "I am pleased to shake your hand".

Some time later, the mind of Sir Humphrey Wonnacott had never been so agile. While Abdullah had been talking, the chairman had been thinking hard, each sentence spoken by the Arab triggering another chain of ideas that had to be assessed, pondered, weighed, pro'd con'd and finally rejected as another wave of intuition flowed through his grey matter.

"Just a minute".

The Arab fell silent as the chairman broke into his discourse and stared questioningly.

Sir Humphrey smiled.

"I've listened to what you've said very carefully my friend but," he leaned back in his chair and made a steeple of his fingers, "there is one small thing you are forgetting".

"Forgetting"

"The potion", stated sir Humphrey.

"What of it?" asked Abdullah, "I have explained that the whole idea of this offer is to use this company to make, promote and sell this potion on the international market".

"That's just it", the chairman beamed at the mystified Arab, "I already have it, my chemists are analysing it, breaking it down, so, with this in mind", he continued smugly, "should we not start this discussion anew? And this time, let's have no mention of my having to vacate my position as chairman eh?"

Abdullah nodded sagely.

"I see what you mean, " he admitted, "But good sir, do you think that this potion, whatever it is supposed to be, is the sole reason for my visit to you? My offer?"

"Whatever it's supposed to be", the chairman gloated "you know damn well what it is. What was it you said? Make, promote, sell on the international market?" he turned to Allenby, "Tell him Tom, tell him he'd better get up earlier in the morning if he wants to put one over on me".

Tom Allenby, until now a silent observer sighed,

"Listen to the man Humphrey", he said quietly, "He's heard from his own people at Whitley Warren, he's not trying to put one over on you, he wants to make you an offer you can't refuse".

"What is this Arabian Mafia? An offer I can't refuse, and what about his people?"

"If I might explain sir", Abdullah butted in, "He means that you should contact your man Craig in Whitley warren, the potion, he spread his hands expressively, it no longer has any bargaining power".

Sir Humphrey swallowed, stared hard at the two of them then switched on his intercom, "Lorraine", he barked, "Get me Whitely warren" then he paused, "No , cancel that, just contact them and say I'm on my way there, now!", he released the switch and continued, !And I think gentlemen you should accompany me, let's sort this out once and for all".

Chapter 12

"Good morning mister Anderson", the words broke the stillness of the morning and Reg turned to see Police Constable Emery dismounting from his bicycle.

"Morning", he replied, "Early aren't you? And why the formality, on duty?"

"Yes Reg, traffic control have been on the radio, reported gypsies or hippie's maybe, a mile or two outside the village, they reckon".

"Gypsies eh?£ commented Anderson, not too interested, "the wife's brewing tea Charlie, would you like a cup before you pedal that thing away?"

The policeman laughed.

"That thing Reg is probably the only remaining police issue bone-shaker in the whole of Essex, and I'll thank you not to take the mickey out of it", he propped the bike against the wall of the Inn and then added, "but I will have a cup of tea, it'll give me energy to ride the damn thing."

"Busy?" asked Emery when he was settled with his drink.

"No" said Anderson. "All right in the bar, but the hotel part isn't doing much", then enquired of his wife, "Is it love?"

"We're not too bad", Mrs Anderson replied, "We've got those Arabs and that nice Mister Craig with his girl-friend".

"Girl –friend?" her husband sounded puzzled, "I thought she was his secretary, come from London with him".

"I don't know", his wife tutted, "for someone in the licensed trade you're not very observant. "Haven't you seen the way they act together? Wouldn't do for a ;policeman Mister Emery, would he?"

"Charlie Mrs A, call me Charlie".

"Oh, all right Charlie," she smiled, "Fancy another cuppa?"

P.C, Emery rose from his seat,

"No thanks, duty calls and all that".

He and Anderson walked from the Inn and stood for a few moments enjoying the early morning sunshine.

"Could be a scorcher today", Anderson shaded

his eyes as he looked along the street.

"Aye", agreed the policeman.

"Charlie?" said Anderson, "It's none of my business but," he paused, then as Emery showed signs of impatience, "It's that plant, you know, the fertiliser works, do you ever hear anything from there?"

"Like what?" asked Emery.

"Don't rightly know", Anderson observed, "but I reckon there's some kind of goings on up there".

"What kind of statement is that to make?" the policeman lifted his bike away from the wall and sat astride it, "Goings on? Is it something I should know about?"

"I don't know for sure", Anderson related the incident of Mrs Manners and Eddy Gates, "And some of the other things I've heard of makes me think there's something weird about the place".

"I was here that night," said P.C.Emery, "I don't recall that happening," he grinned, "Water you say?"

"Aye, water, " said Anderson, "this was in the lounge though, you drink in the bar".

"That's true", the policeman started to pedal then stopped. "Mind you, what you've told me doesn't sound as if it's illegal, but if Eddy Gates is having his wicked way with a good-looking woman then, I'll be drinking in the lounge in future, and I'll bring my own water".
"I'd join you Charlie", Anderson gave a mock sigh, "but I don't think my wife'll let me".
They laughed, then paused and looked towards the end of the village street.
"What was that?", Emery got off his bike and gazed into the distance, "Listen, there it goes again, hoof beats, someone calling?"
"Dunno", said Anderson, "Milkman?"
The policeman cast a withering glare at him, "What's he got, runaway horse? I know our milkman, he just delivers the stuff, he don't shout about it, not at this hour anyway, it's only six-o-clock".
"No", said Anderson "But I…what the hell's that?"
That…was a horse and rider approaching at speed along the village street.
"It's another of them Arabs", continued Anderson, "watch it Charlie, he's coming

straight at us".

The Arab, in flowing robes, pulled his mount to halt in front of the Inn, swung an ornate rifle in a flamboyant arc and fired a rapid three shots into the air.

Anderson leapt for cover as the reports ached in the quiet street and a raucous cloud of crows winged noisily upwards cawing their annoyance.

"Here", emery dropped the bike to the ground and took out his note-book, "Have you got a licence for that fire-arm? Don't you know it's an offence to discharge a weapon on the public highway? Get off that horse my lad and hand me your gun".

The Arab uttered a string of unintelligible words and sat, obviously awaiting a reply.

"Get down I say", emery repeated authoritively, "I confiscate that rifle in the name of the law".

"I don't think he understands you Charlie", Anderson sidled from the doorway he had taken refuge in and tugged at the policeman's sleeve, "shall I get one of the Arabs to translate?"

"Good idea", said the policeman, "and you,

Charlie Emery pointed at the horseman, "you stay, compre? Wait here", his hands made shapes in the air as he tried to explain what he intended to do "We fetch other man to speak", in an aside to Reg Anderson, he asked, "who are you getting!"

"Well", said Anderson, "Two of them came in last night but I don't know about that Ben Acate bloke, haven't seen him for a day or two".

"Ben Acate"

The men stared as the Arab hissed the name, spat fiercely on the ground, narrowly missing the policeman's foot as he did so, then they took an involuntary step backwards as he screamed something in Arabic to the high heavens, wheeled his mount and galloped swiftly away.

"Come back here" shouted Emery, grabbing his bicycle and attempting to follow.

"You won't catch him Charlie".

Emery got off his bike again.

"You're right Reg. I've got no chance there, still, I'll contact headquarters, I'm not having some foreigner letting his gun off on my patch", he busied himself with the radio then paused as from somewhere in the distance came the sound of another shot, then a veritable salvo. The two men stared at each other.

"Do you think it's a war or something?"

"Dunno"

Villagers began to appear from their cottages and Emery and Anderson were soon surrounded by people demanding to know what had disrupted their slumber. Then came voices, shouting , more shots, the noise of wheels rumbling and rattling along the tarmacked road. Silence fell on the group outside the Hotel and the other villagers stood as if they were lining the street as for a march-past which it seemed to be, for, even as they watched, the street began to fill with animals, whining, barking dogs, sheep, goats, the whole bleating, baaing mass escorted by black-clad women brandishing sticks and calling shrilly in an attempt to control the heaving carpet of livestock.

Arab men strolled behind, smiling to the onlookers and waving nonchalantly to all and sundry.

Riders came, their ornate headdresses and burnous flowing as they trotted gracefully along the thoroughfare, and the noise, the incredible, cacophonous discord of harsh voices rising above the din of the animals and the increasing tinkling and banging of pots and pans that swung haphazardly from the tailgates of the wagons that followed the four-legged horde into the main street of Whitley Warren and filled it to capacity.

Then camels. Stately beasts that strode imperiously along the pavement and street alike, making their own progress through the seething mass. No royal procession could have matched the regal mien of these creatures, their disdainful gaze and the occasional coughing ejection of phlegm making several of the watchers wipe hastily at their faces as the well-aimed spit found it's mark.

Police constable Charles Emery stood transfixed as the cavalcade passed before his astounded eyes, and it wasn't finished...

A short lull was immediately followed by a fusillade of shots and miraculously a space appeared as the crowd surged towards the pavements. Another body of horsemen galloped at full tilt down the village street, pulled their sweating mounts to a halt then shouted an exultant welcome as a finely decorated carriage, drawn by four of the blackest horses the policeman had ever seen, drew up before the entrance of the hotel.

From behind the P.C. and Anderson there appeared in the doorway the sheikh's sons, Tariq and his brother Ali. The sight of them brought another burst of firing from the mounted Arabs.

"Stop that immediately", commanded Emery, with all the authority of the law in his tone, but it was to no avail, it was doubtful whether he was even heard above the incessant clamour.

Then the carriage door opened and one Arab swung from his horse to prostrate himself on the ground as the Sheikh of Sheikhs, the leader of the Kohani emerged from the dim interior of the carriage, made a token gesture of stepping on the head of the recumbent and then lifted a hand of acknowledgement as the crowd burst into another round of cheering and shouting as they welcomed their ruler. As the sheikh embraced his two sons, his personal bodyguards formed a half circle between his person and the frustrated Police Constable Emery who was leaping up and down screaming.

"That's it, that's it, you're nicked, you're all nicked!"

He was still mumbling the words as Reg Anderson lead him inside the hotel and sat him down with a large whiskey.

"Drink that Charlie", he said compassionately, then turned as a voice asked,

"Is that one of the local policemen?"

"He is our local policeman, our only one", he stared at the man who had spoken, "Who are you?"

"Immigration", the man replied then to Emery, "Haven't your people organised anything yet?" The policeman's glazed expression didn't convey much of an answer so the man continued,

"Obviously not!"

"What's going on?" asked Anderson, "Charlie's a bit upset, he can't talk".

"I can see that, and I appreciate that these events might seem a little odd to your good self but, without my appearing to be rude, I don't think this matter concerns you for the moment," his tone verged on the mysterious as he added, "suffice to say that this is as far as they go".
"Who?"
Anderson's question hung on the empty air for the stranger had walked swiftly into the room.

Emily Lang sat close to Andrew on the settee in the lounge of the hotel and he inched away. She moved until her thigh touched his then smiled broadly as he again made space between them.
"Andrew", she grasped his arm, "Are you making out that you don't like it?"
"It's not that Emily", he answered, "But you're always doing something when there's people around".
"So what?" she said, "Haven't you got over your inhibitions yet? No –one's watching us, they've got their own business to attend to, besides,"

she leaned over and kissed him, "It's a free country!"

"Emily", he scolded mildly, and then blushed, but he couldn't help giving a half-smile as he pulled his head away, "You're a wanton hussy".

Emily sidled closer and stroked his leg,

"Am I hussy enough for you?" she whispered.

Andrew leapt from the settee and took a pace forward before turning and saying sternly,

"Now look what you've done", he ignored her merry laugh as he pulled his jacket down in an attempt to hide his growing erection.

Suddenly he sat down again as Peter Winfield approached and said,

"Hello you two, not at the plant then?"

"To do what?" asked Andrew, "we've been calling for the last couple of days after we helped to clean up, haven't we Emily?"

She nodded as he continued, "I don't even know what's supposed to be happening at the precious plant".

"Forgive me ", said Winfield, "I thought you were supposed to be the Boss-man and Boss-men should be where the work is, right?"

Andrew sighed.

"I don't know about being in charge, when sir Humphrey hears what's been going on I don't think I'll be even keeping my old job."

"Haven't you contacted him?"

Andrew shook his head and sighed afresh,

"It's not for the want of trying though, I was on the phone for hours yesterday, I don't know what I'm supposed to do".

"Day before", Emily interrupted.

"Day before then", he agreed, "Still I couldn't get through whatever day it was".

"Didn't you try from the hotel here?"

Winfield took in Andrew's embarrassed stare and shook his own head, "No, obviously not, you were probably too busy, those Arab fellers got through to the London office, you didn't try that one either?"

Andrew smiled sheepishly and Winfield tutted, "oh well never mind, who are those Arabs anyway? Do they work for you as well as Ben Acate?"

"No", said Andrew, then turned to Emily for support, "They just appeared out of the blue didn't they?"

"Yes", agreed Emily, "but in view of what happened, it's a good thing they did turn up, especially that one with the hose".

Winfield laughed.

"That was a scream," he said, "I didn't see the first bit, but I was , er, otherwise engaged, mind you there was a lot going on while that pong was in everybody's nostrils."

Andrew snorted.

"Hmmph", then, "I thought it was disgusting what I saw of it all", he stared accusingly at Emily, "What certain people were doing!"

She coloured red.

"It affected everybody", she said defensively, "There was an excuse, it…"

"It didn't affect me", Andrew stated,

"Come to think of it", said Winfield, "you're right, it didn't affect you, so why was that?"

Emily stared.

"That's true Andrew", she observed, "Even in the corridor with that dog around you, I felt it, but you…"

"What dog?" asked Winfield, "something I missed?"

"When I was being introduced to the staff",

began Andrew , then , "Oh never mind it was nothing anyway".

"Nothing it might have been", persisted Emily, "But why didn't the smell get to you? Everyone else suffered".

"Ha-ha", guffawed Winfield, "I wouldn't call that suffering".

Just then, Reg Anderson came over to them, "Mister Craig, there's a message from the fertiliser place, would you get up there right away, sir Humphrey is on his way from London".

"What?" Andrew sprang to his feet, "Emily, Sir Humphrey!"

"Calm yourself", she stood also and took his arm, "I told you before, he's only a man".

"Shall I tell them you're on your way?" Anderson patiently awaited a reply.

"Someone's still on the phone?" asked Winfield and as Anderson nodded, "I'll speak to them, you two get yourselves organised and ," as he walked off with Anderson, "don't go without me, I need a lift."

Emily lifted a hand in acknowledgement then turned to Andrew.

"Come on love, let's get the car, and don't worry it's not the end of the world."

Doctor Bryant hastened out to welcome Sir Humphrey Wonnacott as he saw the limousine sweep into the parking area.
Reaching it, he realised it was Emily Lang driving.
"Oh, it's you lot", he remarked dolefully.
"Who did you expect?" asked Winfield, emerging from the rear seat, "We've just come from the village at your special request".
"Yes I know", Bryant nodded, "But Sir Humphrey could turn up at any minute and the way he sounded, he's out for blood".
Andrew's face whitened as he and Emily got out of the car and he heard the Doctor's words.
"He didn't happen to mention who's blood did he?"
Bryant shook his head as Emily said, "Come on Andrew no one can blame you for what happened".
"I suppose not", Andrew didn't sound too sure, "I did try and phone him, several times".

"Not your fault Craig" said the Doctor, "The exchange was out, all that water, soaked whatever makes the damn thing work and my phone was the only one you could get out on".

"Most interesting", commented Winfield, "but, why are we here? Do we stand in line and form a guard of honour for his nibs?"

"Don't be silly Peter", Bryant turned away, "Let's go to my office, have a coffee while we're waiting".

"Coffee", muttered Andrew sotto-voce, "That seems to be the limit of Doctor Bryant's planning doesn't it?"

"You can't say that", Winfield took it upon himself to defend the good doctor. "When the plant was in full swing, we drank whiskey in his office" he sighed at the recollection, "things are tight now though, we can't afford it anymore".

Many cups of coffee later, past midnight in fact, Bryant admitted that perhaps the chairman wasn't arriving just yet.

"Emily and I will go back to the hotel" said Andrew.

"I don't think you should", Bryant stated."Not

yet anyway".

"If it gets any later we'll be sleeping here", commented Emily.

"Yeah, I suppose you'll be wanting those blankets I've got in the stores eh?"Winfield laughed as Bryant shot him a withering glance.

"Is that what we're doing?" asked Emily, "Sleeping here?"

"Would it hurt it?" Bryant was almost begging, "It might not be all night, Sir Humphrey did say he'd be here presently".

"Appears to me our gaffer says quite a lot", observed Winfield, "Don't mean that it's all gospel though".

They fell silent as they looked at each other then Bryant asked quietly, "Well!"

Chapter 13

Early next morning Sir Humphrey arrived. After spending an almost sleepless night in the few armchairs they had found, it was a weary bunch of people that gathered for some life-giving coffee in Doctor Bryant's room.

He himself sat staring out of the window and hardly had time to recognise the chairman's car before the vehicle swept to a halt with a crunch of gravel and footsteps came clattering along the corridor and up the stairs.

Bryant motioned to Winfield to open the door, but even as his assistant stared uncomprehendingly at his gesture, the portal burst open to admit Sir Humphrey Wonnacott, Tom Allenby, and the Arab, Abdullah Karim.

"What the hells' been going on here? Snarled Sir Humphrey.

The question hung unanswered as everyone looked uncomfortably at each other.

Andrew felt Emily's hand on his, and returned

her grip as he stood up slowly, bringing her to her feel also.

I, I," he began haltingly, "I, er, take full responsibility for everything", he stated, "Yes, I do, you put me in charge and it is therefore incumbent upon me to assume..."

"Stop waffling Craig", the chairman interrupted, then to Bryant, "what's happened to my potion?"

"Excuse me sir", now it was Abdullah's turn to interrupt, "By saying your potion, you do mean the item that was stolen from the Kohani and by right should be returned to them".

Sir Humphrey cast a withering glance in his direction but his voice was controlled as he said,

"Don't split hairs over whose potion it is eh? It's a trifle late for that seeing the bloody stuff's gone".

"Gone", queried Winfield, then the phone chose that moment to ring and all attention was focussed on the instrument.

The ringing continued until the chairman asked sarcastically,

"Is it possible that someone could answer that

damn thing, or do we all stand round like a campanologist's convention admiring the sound of the bell".

"Sorry, sorry", Bryant picked up the receiver, spoke for a few moments then held the handset out to Sir Humphrey, "I think you ought to deal with this sir".

"Fool", the chairman snatched the telephone, "Can't you handle anything?" then into the receiver, "Yes, yes I am the boss as you so quaintly put it, yes, yes...", his face ran a gamut of emotion as he fell silent and all eyes fixed on him. At last the chairman sat down, still clasping the phone and said weakly to Abdullah Karim, "Do you know a Sheikh? I didn't catch his name", then the Arab shrugged,

"well it seems as if it's your problem if you do know him, he's only landed the whole of his bloody tribe here, women, tents, animals, the..." he listened to the phone again, "No, they aren't here at my invitation, I don't know any Arabs, hold on, I've got a chap with me who can sort it out for you", he thrust the phone at Karim.

"What was that sir? Asked Bryant, "Trouble?"
"Trouble", the chairman gave a hollow laugh, "Not really, we've only been invaded by Arabs. That was the immigration people saying that the police stopped them in the village, they said they were coming to see me! How the hell do they know me?

"They've er, come to England sir?" asked Andrew brightly.

"Don't you listen?" the chairman said angrily, "They're here in Whitley Warren".

"I must go", stated Abdullah Karim as he replaced the telephone.

"Eh?" the chairman looked at him, "What do you mean, go? We've got things to discuss".

"Forgive me", the Arab was apologetic, "As you heard the Sheikh has travelled to England and brought the Kohani to your village, officials are at this moment trying to arrest the whole tribe, I must go".

"So it is your lot?" Sir Humphrey said, "Right", he touched Andrew on the shoulder, "In that case young Craig here will go with you", he addressed the accountant, "Get along with him, see what's happening and report back to me personally, And I mean, to me by phone, by carrier pigeon if need be, I don't care, let me know what's going on, right?"

"Right" said Andrew, "Emily?"

"You don't have to take your woman everywhere do you?"

"She's not my woman as you so crudely put it", said Andrew, anger in his voice.

The chairman stared undaunted, Andrew continued, "In fact I resent you speaking so disparagingly about Miss Lang", Sir Humphrey gazed uncomprehendingly at Craig's rebellion and he took heart from the chairman's silence, "She's not my woman, she is..," now Emily hung onto his words, "My fiancée!"

"Oh Andrew", she kissed him fiercely as the chairman said,

"Well that's isn't a turn up for the books Tom, isn't it"?

"It is Humphrey", Tom Allenby smiled, "Congratulations to you both".

"Yes, congratulations", echoed the chairman, "But I'm paying you two , you're on my time so, for the moment could you please leave him alone Madam? Let him go to the village with this chap and find out what's happening there."

Red faced, they broke their embrace and Andrew said,

"I'm going sir", his eyes fixed on Emily's and he straightened as she gave him a smile of encouragement, threw what he considered to be a intimidating glare at the chairman, then strode proudly from the room in the wake of Abdullah Karim.

"Right," Sir Humphrey rubbed his hands as he crossed to the window, "Break out the drinks now that's settled and let's talk".

"Er, yes certainly", Bryant hurried to the kettle and asked, "Sugar?"

"Sugar?" the chairman looked askance, "What do you mean, sugar?"

"In your coffee sir!"

"Coffee? Haven't you got a proper drink?" he addressed Tom Allenby, "they haven't got a drink Tom", he tutted then turned to Peter Winfield, "You there, you're?"

"Winfield" Peter volunteered.

"That's right, I pride myself on knowing the names of my staff", he ignored the man's action as the chemist raised his eyes to the ceiling in mock disgust and continued,

"Winfield, be a good chap and nip down to the motor, there's a bottle of brandy in the boot, it is open."

"What, the brandy?"

The others smiled as the chairman shot a glance at Winfield.

"Brandy? What are you talking about?"

Disconcerted under the chairman's gaze, Peter Winfield hastened to explain,

"The brandy sir, you said it was open?"

"Open", Sir Humphrey looked at Allenby, then at Bryant, Emily stepped forward.

"It was a joke sir, you said fetch the brandy from the car, it's open".

"And so it is young lady, I rarely lock the boot".

"It's a play on words Humphrey", Tom Allenby informed him.

"Oh," Sir Humphrey considered that then, in a dejected voice said, "Thank you for that explanation, not , doesn't that make you understand why I'm so uptight lately?" his voice became louder and his arms stretched out to indicate everyone in the room, "I'm surrounded by bloody idiots, you," looking at Winfield, "do you realise the pressure I'm under? I'm trying to save your job, and you make jokes?" he shook his head in disbelief. "Just do me a favour Winfield, fetch the brandy", he pointed through the window as he spoke then swore, "What the hell's going on now?"

Everyone moved to join Sir Humphrey at the window and saw Andrew and the Arab standing by the car that they had driven up from Whitley Warren,

"What's wrong?" asked Allenby.

"Those two", the chairman pointed, "Look".

The others dutifully looked, then Emily said, "Andrew can't drive sir".

The chairman stared hard at her, his face mottling with a suppressed anger,

"Yes, now you mention it, I remember. The man can't drive, but tell me Miss?"

"Lang", she offered

"oh yes, well Miss Lang, surely the Arab can drive?" as she shrugged to signify her ignorance of Abdullah Karim's capabilities, Sir Humphrey, without taking his eyes off her, asked Allenby, "Tom, that Arab drives a car doesn't he?"

"Dunno Humphrey, he came with us, you drove".

The chairman was livid but contented himself with shouting through the open window, "Craig", the two men looked up, "I realise that you're in no hurry to get to the village", then he almost screamed, "But I could have walked there in the time you're taking".

The Arab and Andrew stared at each other then at the figure leaning precariously from the office window,

"I can't drive", called Andrew.

"I know that you bloody cretin", retorted the chairman, "Give the keys to the Arab, let him drive".

"Sir", Emily tugged at the chairman's coat.

"In a minute", Sir Humphrey snapped.

"But sir", she persisted

"I said in a minute" , the chairman straightened as he turned, then his face changed colour as he saw what she was holding, "Tha...that's a set of car keys!"

"Yes sir",

"What are you doing with them?"

"It's the keys to the car sir, if you remember; I'm the one who you told to drive Mister Craig and Ben Acate down here".

"She's right Humphrey", Tom Allenby supported Emily's statement.

The chairman took a deep breath, then to everyone's surprise, spoke quite normally and controlled,

"So you've got the car keys my dear. Well, would you please continue your driving duties and take Mister Craig and the other gentleman to Whitley Warren", he felt behind him for Bryant's chair and slumped into it, "And Winfield my friend, please fetch the brandy, because of ever a man needed a drink, then I do , right now".

"So much for that", commented Peter Winfield as he and Emily walked long the corridor, then as she nodded, "Every time I see that man I want to give him a piece of my mind".

"He's a pig", stated Emily.

"He's our chief unfortunately".

"It doesn't make him any less of a pig", she halted Winfield with a hand on his arm, "you should try working for him, the way he treats everybody, especially Andrew".

"I do work for him", laughed Peter, "mind you we don't see a lot of him down here, or we didn't until then potion thing started, Oh that remind me", he started to walk again and she fell into step with him, "I'll stop off at the lab, your Andrew might as well have what's left of the stuff, it's only a few drops, but I don't want it hanging round", he winked, "you never know what effect it might have on people".

Emily blushed.

"Don't remind me, I bet there's a few like me who, well, you know".

"I do know", said Winfield feelingly, "why do you think I said it?"

Going into the lab, he gave Emily a small bottle and she wrapped it in her handkerchief before placing it carefully in her pocket.

AS they emerged from the building, Peter Winfield looked towards the window of Doctor Bryant's office.

"Just checking the old man isn't watching from above".

Emily smiled grimly but didn't answer until

they reached the car,

"Run your little errand Peter", she said facetiously, then to Andrew, "I'm driving you two to the village, our boss says so".

Winfield opened the boot of Sir Humphrey's car and took out the brandy he found there.

"I'll put poison in it", he shouted after Emily as she drove off.

They were well on the road before Andrew asked,

"Poison? What did he mean?"

"A joke", Emily answered, then sighed, "Only a joke".

"Sir Humphrey is not a good master?"

Emily stared at the reflection of the Arab in the rear-view mirror but left it to Andrew to reply,

"No, I mean yes, he's not our master, we work for him, but, well, it's not that he's cruel, in fact he put me in charge of this operation".

"In charge", Emily's tone was mocking,

"Yes, in charge, didn't I have the potion?"

Abdullah attended his words closely,

"You had it? My friends say it was wasted, with some unfortunate effects, you are a chemist?"

"A chemist? No," answered Andrew, "I am an

accountant".

Abdullah nodded sagely.

"In my country, especially with men such as the Prince, accountants are worthy of great honour and are held in high esteem".

"Are they really?" Andrew preened himself, silent for a moment with the thought of him being in the middle-east, feted by some oil-rich prince, with one stroke of his pen making razor sharp decisions that would place millions of dollars here, and there, leaving tax officials wondering just how they could combat the infinite variations of control that this famous accountant displayed.

"what's that"? asked Emily suddenly.

Disturbed from his reverie, Andrew looked through the windscreen and saw a crowd of people in the road along with several police cars and a small queue of driverless vehicles. Pulling up behind the rear car, Emily wound down her window as a harassed-looking policeman approached,

"Sorry Miss, you'll have to go back, Whitley Warren is out of bounds".

"that's where we're going," stated Emily firmly.

"That's where you're wrong," countered the policeman, "the village is out of bounds, closed to traffic, it's also under quarantine, there's a load of foreigners there and they've got animals and all sorts with them, so we can't let anyone through. The immigration are there, customs are there, and the police are there, and me being one of the police, I'm telling you officially that you can't go on so turn around and go home".

"It is our home", said Andrew, sticking his head out of the side window, "we live in the hotel and this gentleman is on his way to sort things out".

The policeman stared, then opened the rear door and asked Abdullah to step out.

"Is this true?", then as the Arab nodded, "and could I ask who you are sir?"

As Abdullah Karim explained that he was the official representative of the Kohani, the policeman spoke into his radio.

"No need for that sir", the constable finished his conversation and waved away the proffered plastic-coated card, printed in Arabic and bearing a picture of Abdullah Karim, "You may continue on your journey, my superiors are waiting for you in Whitley Warren".

"Thank you officer" said the Arab as he rejoined Andrew in the car.

"Lucky you had your diplomatic pass", observed Andrew as they drove away.

"Yes," answered Abdullah not mentioning that the document was in fact his membership card for the Kuwaiti Golf club.

Chapter 14

The village hotel was jammed solid with high ranking army officers, policeman, sober-suited gentlemen from various departments of Her Majesty's Government, and a well satisfied Reg Anderson leaned against the bar nursing a large whiskey. The bar was doing incredible business and the kitchen reported an overwhelming demand for meals, sandwiches, tea and coffee.

"Lovely isn't it?" remarked Mrs. Anderson as she busied herself serving.

"Certainly is", replied Reg, "how are we for stock?"

"We've never done so well," stated his wife, "I've emptied the till twice already".

"What about stock though?" persisted Reg.

"No problem", his wife served another round of drinks, "the food is virtually finished, but we've lots of beer and spirits and when you're ready you can drive to that supermarket in…"

"Don't be stupid woman", Reg drained his glass in one swallow and grimaced as the fiery liquid burnt his throat.

"I'm waiting", said Mrs. Anderson threateningly,

"for what?" asked the bewildered hotelier.

"for you to tell me why it's stupid to refurbish our stocks so we can sell more food to these people".

Reg seeing the anger on his wife's face spoke carefully.

"We're cut off love, no one can leave", he made a gesture towards the crowded lounge, "this lot didn't turn up to eat us out of house and home, nice though it is, it's the Arabs that brought them here".

"Yes, well", Mrs. Anderson mulled over her husband's words, but loath to let him get away with his remarks said, "People got to eat though".

"Of course, what I'm saying is if our grub's gone then they've had it, by the way, we eat as well you know".

"We've got stuff", she said curtly as she moved away to serve another customer.

Reg sighed as he surveyed the mass of people, then stepped forward and tapped a police officer on the shoulder,

"Excuse me, could you tell me what's happening please?"

"You're er?"

"Anderson", he supplied, "Manager here, well, owner actually".

The policeman stared at him,

"Yes sir, well, there are no developments as yet, but I hear that a senior Arab official is on his way. After he arrives I'll probably be in a better position to give more information to you and the residents".

"Of the hotel?"

"Of the village sir," the policeman's tone hardened, "you're not the only one to suffer inconvenience".

"Of course", Anderson, embarrassed, thanked the officer and moved off into the crowd.

The car bearing Andrew and his companions had just passed the Whitley Warren sign-post when Emily said resignedly,

"Oh no, not again".

She pulled the car to a halt beside a red-faced army sergeant who stood with four other khaki clad figures making a human barricade in the road.

"Everybody out", said the sergeant as Emily wound down her window.

"Excuse me" said Andrew, "We've got permission to go into the village, there's people waiting to see this Arab gentleman".

"I'm sure there is sir" and I'm not stopping you," the army man held the door open as Emily alighted.

"What do you mean?" asked Andrew as he and Abdullah got out also.

"I mean you carry on sir, see who you like", he beckoned to one of his men, "It's your car we're stopping, the village is chock-a-block with traffic and who knows what else", he grinned, "So you'll have to walk from here". Turning to a soldier he said, "Park this one with the others", then to Emily, "give us your name miss, I'll label your keys and when this fuss is over you can pick them up from our headquarters".

They watched their car being driven into a field

where several others stood, then turned to go on their way.

"Is that it?" asked Andrew of no-one in particular as they began to walk along the road.

"Listen" Emily said suddenly.

Andrew stared at Emily, then at Karim as the Arab smiled broadly and began to walk faster, then he heard the noise himself. A drone almost musical, no tune that he knew though, then more distinctly, the bleating of sheep, cattle lowing and voices, men's, women's, that sounded foreign even from a distance, laughter. Emily quickened her pace and Andrew stepped out to join her and Abdullah as they rounded a bend in the road.

"Good Lord", Emily breathed as the three of them halted.

Ahead was parked an army vehicle that, with a police panda car formed a make-shift road block. A couple of soldiers chatted idly with a policeman, and beyond them Andrew could see that the street was filled with people, Arabs strolled about in their flowing robes, ignoring the stares of the small groups of villagers that stood here and there. The green in front of the hotel had several tents pitched on it and, even in the warm sunshine, fires had been lit and they smoked away as Arab women went about the business of cooking.

Sheep, goats and horse even, roamed freely, and as Andrew looked on in amazement, he saw, tethered to lamp-posts, car bumpers and what seemed to be any convenient hitching place, camels, lots and lots of camels.

"Look at that", breathed Andrew, awestruck.

"Smell that", commented Emily, wrinkling her nose.

Abdullah said nothing, but his eyes sparkled as he ushered them into a walk.

"Hold on there", called the policeman as he came toward them.

"Yes", said Abdullah.

"If your name is Karim then I'm to escort you to the hotel" said the policeman.

"Officer", Abdullah spoke as if to a child a he indicated the crowded street, "I think that an escort, however well intentioned, would be rather out of place, these are my people".

Crestfallen at the Arab's gentle rebuke, the

constable fell back and allowed Abdullah Karim and his two companions to continue their progress.

At the fertiliser plant, Sir Humphrey sat glowering as he listened to Bryant's account of what had occurred from the time the potion had been spilled. There was silence as the others waited for his expected outburst, then the chairman took a swallow of brandy, and surprisingly laughed, a hearty guffaw that developed into a fit of coughing. He gasped, coughed again, and as everyone stared blankly, wondering how to take this strange attitude, and the even stranger sound of laughter coming from the chairman's bearded lips, Tom Allenby sprang forward and thumped Sir Humphrey smartly on the back. This triggered the other two into action and, as the chairman alternately laughed and coughed, Bryant and Winfield joined with Allenby and began to pummel the chairman with a hearty enthusiasm that threatened the poor fellow with a lasting injury.

Struggling to his feet, the scarlet faced Sir Humphrey waved frantic arms in an attempt to protect himself from the well-intentioned blows and eventually found his voice.

"Get off me", he squawked, then louder, "What the hell are you trying to do, murder me?"

"You were choking", said Allenby.

"That's no bloody reason for knocking me about like that, or is that what you're after? Not content with stealing Farm Chemicals from under my nose, you want to kill me off as well!"

"Rubbish Humphrey", Allenby was annoyed, "don't start that again, you know we're in a vulnerable position and I'm just interested in getting what we can out of it before we all go down the pan".

"Ah", the chairman sneered, "the truth is coming out now is it? Get what you can eh?"

"I don't mean that", Tom Allenby searched for words, "It's, well, it's a whole different set-up isn't it, we already know we won't survive a vote of no-confidence at the board meeting so it's only sensible to look at the situation from a mercenary point of view".

"Oh yes", persisted the chairman, "Mercenary

is the right word all right, I only wonder why I never noticed this trait in you before now, perhaps I'd never have made you my Managing Director".

"Excuse me", Bryant and Winfield had listened to the exchange with interest and now Bryant spoke, "do I understand that you're saying the firm is finished?"

"What about our jobs?" Winfield added.

"There's no danger to your jobs", said Allenby, "in fact you might even be better off under new management".

"Yes, look after the peasants", Sir Humphrey chipped in, "It's only the top man who's destined for the chop, the bloke who's led you all and made sure there was a job for you to go to".

"So what would you like to do now sir?" Doctor Bryant changed the subject with the subtlety of a sledge-hammer, "inspect the premises? You haven't seen the new labs, the changes in the offices.."

"What's the good of that", interrupted Sir Humphrey, "the potion is all gone".

"It's not all gone", Winfield stressed the 'all'.

There was a silence then the chairman said quietly ,
"Not gone?"
"No", Winfield could have bitten his tongue as he saw the relief spread over the chairman's face. The least he could do for Sir Humphrey the better he would have liked it, still, he'd done it now, "No there was some left, I put it in a bottle".
"Did you now?" Sir Humphrey smirked, "Hear that Tom, he's put it in a bottle, how's your friend Alley-ben-oop going to take that eh? No bargaining power? Who's got no bargaining power? That's great news", he turned to Winfield, "Well done , where is it , in your laboratory?"
"No", Winfield stood as the chairman questioned him.
"Well, spit it out, where have you got it?"
"I haven't got it".
"You've just this minute told me you've got the potion".
"not all of it, a little drop that was left after the, er, accident".
"then where is it?" screamed the chairman

losing his patience.

"I gave it to Emily Lang to give to Craig".

"You what? The pair of them are in the village with the Arab, he'll get it".

"Not necessarily", Tom Allenby attempted to placate the chairman, "Craig probably won't even think about it".

"I hope not", the chairman turned to Winfield, "for your bloody sake I hope not".

Stung into a reply, Winfield said huffily,

"I'm sorry but if you told people that it was such a close secret I would have kept it in the lab".

The chairman stared and was about to say something more when the telephone rang.

"That's them," cried Sir Humphrey, "I'll get it".

He snatched up the phone and barked a sharp "Hello", into the mouthpiece.

The others watched as his attitude changed, he slumped into the chair and held the instrument out to Allenby, "You speak to her Tom, it's Lorraine, about the board meeting".

Tom Allenby took the proffered handset and spoke in length to sir Humphrey's secretary. Bryant and Winfield remained silent though they couldn't resist the odd glance at the chairman as he sat brooding.

Eventually Allenby replaced the receiver and said brightly,

"That's it Humphrey, back to London, though we'll have to contact Abdullah Karim first, there's got to be a time limit on any offer he wants to make. Three days, a week?" he stopped as he saw Sir Humphrey shaking his head, "Longer? Shorter? You've got to give him chance otherwise there's nothing concrete to put before the board".

"No", said Sir Humphrey emphatically, "definitely not!"

"I don't understand, surely the Arab is a way out for the firm?"

"I'm not interested in the bloody Arab", the chairman banged a fist on the desktop, "It's your bloody board meeting, and I'm not going to be there".

"But Humphrey…"

"But nothing, listen Tom. If you think that I'm going to throw myself on the so-called mercy of a bunch of idiots that I've made rich over the years, then you've got another think coming.

For God's sake man, I'm the boss of this outfit, I made it, I made you and the board, and I can't go to London and act like a little boy having his wrist smacked for being naughty".

"I know what you mean Humphrey," said Tom Allenby, "but don't you realise, this is the end whether you're there or not, there'll be papers to sign, a lot of sorting out".

"Right", the chairman stood up, "I'll travel to London with you, I'll even sign the papers, but I'm not going anywhere near that meeting and you," he addressed the words at Bryant but his eyes included Peter Winfield, "See if you can do something right for a change, Get hold of that Arab bloke and tell him he's got two days to finalise an offer, and Winfield, please don't breathe a word about potions, just tell him to get his details in writing and come to London with them, two days, right?"

"Right" said Bryant as Winfield nodded in agreement. The chairman and Allenby walked from the office, then Sir Humphrey came back in.

"That's mine", he remarked, and a wicked grin spread across his face as he picked up the brandy bottle and left the room.

"Tight bastard", Winfield muttered.

Chapter 15

"Psst"

Through the hubbub Andrew heard the noise, "Psst" I was repeated and he looked about him. "something wrong?" asked Emily, but didn't pursue the question as Andrew shook his head.

Abdullah Karim halted as an Arab greeted him and they began to converse animatedly as Andrew and Emily walked on.

"Psst". This time an urgent hiss that stopped Andrew in his tracks. He scanned the faces around him as he called to Emily.

"I heard it again"

"Heard what?"

Before he could answer, a hooded figure sidled close and grasped his arm,

"Mister Craig, it is I. I need your help", the cover slipped from the swarthy visage of...

"Ben Acate", gasped Emily.

"Hush pretty lady", he murmured, "My very life

is in danger, quickly follow me".

He led them up the side of the hotel and into a yard. Stacks of crates formed an alleyway through which the Arab scuttled with Andrew and Emily following.

They halted in a shelter between the stacks where Ben Acate threw the robe from his shoulders and sat on a single box that served as a chair.

"Mister Craig, Miss Emily," he beamed, "You don't know how glad I am to see you, Please, sit", he indicated two upturned beer barrels, "It is not what I would like to offer you but unfortunately it is all I have at this time"

"But what are you doing here?" asked Andrew, "Where have you been?"

The Arab shrugged.

"Where could I go?" he stood up, "I have brought shame and disgrace on myself and my Sheikh, why? I do not know. It is only that at the time it seemed as if it were right, but now..."

"how can we help?" Emily interrupted, "We have no power over the law, if you're arrested for stealing, what can we do?"

Ben Acate laughed, a hollow sound that bore no resemblance to mirth,

"If it were only that easy dear lady, arrested, it is not that I fear", he paused, "You see, if Tariq, or even Ali, the Sheikh's sons" he added as the others stared at him inquiringly, "if they were to see me", he grimaced and made a stabbing motion at his chest.

"You mean…?"

"Kill you?" Emily finished Andrew's question. Ben Acate nodded as a solitary tear rolled down his whiskery cheek.

Emily rose and placed an arm around his shoulder.

"We will help you".

"Oh Miss Emily", Ben Acate planted a swift kiss on the lips of the astonished woman.

"hold on", said Andrew, "there's no need for that".

"My apologies", Ben Acate sounded repentant, "but I am so grateful".

"Have you been here all the time?" asked Emily.

"No", said the Arab, "I was able to stay in the hotel, until Tariq and Ali…." he paused.

"It must have been a shock when you saw them at the factory, especially when the place was being flooded".

"A shock indeed Mister Craig, and now the Kohani are here, How? Maybe a miracle, but seeing them was a shock of shocks, I looked from my window and there they were. Unbelievable!" The Arab shook his head to show how unbelievable it was.

"How can we help?" said Emily

"Ah", Ben Acate sat on the crate again, "I could hide until the Kohani leave your country, as they must do shortly, for I have heard your government people say this".

"That's simple then", said Emily, "Hide. You can get a train to London from here, no-one would find you in London".

"no", the Arab spoke sadly, "my conscience would never let me rest and because of this you must intercede with my chieftain, the Sheikh. Tell him how grievously I have wronged him, how I suffer mental tortures beyond all imagination knowing that I stole the secret potion of the Kohani", Ben Acate leapt to his feet, "As Allah is my judge, tell him", the

words became a guttural Arabic and he shouted aloud then sinking to his knees, he ripped open his shirt sending buttons everywhere, and held out his hands in a plea of supplication, "Speak for me Mister Craig, Miss Emily, tell the Sheikh, my master, I am bereft".
"You're mad", said Andrew.
"Well", said Emily, "if you feel like that, I'm not sure we can see the gentleman", she looked at Andrew, "What do you think?"
"I think he's a lunatic", he answered, "but we'd better help him somehow, we can't see him killed, though that seems a bit strong".
"should we come back to you here?" asked Emily.
"Kind lady", Ben Acate stood, "You do this for me, I kiss your feet, I kiss Mister Craig's feet".
"Not likely", said Andrew, "now tell me, if we see your Sheikh, how will you know?"
"I will see you", said the Arab, "I have stayed too long in this place, but I will be close, and will know when you have spoken to my master", he led them from the yard then faded back into the piles of crates.
"Strange", said Emily as they made their way

to the main street.

"Strange indeed", answered Andrew, "But let's find this Abdullah chap and see if I can telephone Sir Humphrey to tell him what's happening".

"what a racket", she mouthed, and it certainly was. The noise from the Arabs was overpowering, the din of the animals vying with the shouts and cries of the Kohani as they went about their business.

"Mister Craig", Reg Anderson called to them from the hotel. "Are you coming in for a drink?" then as they neared him, "I had to let your rooms go unfortunately, but those two Arabs have moved into the tents so you can have their rooms and", he didn't finish for at that moment a chorus of shouting drew their attention to where Abdullah Karim was standing with a group of Kohani.

"I think he wants you", Emily touched Andrew's arm, "He's beckoning".

"You come as well Emily"

"To hold your hand?"

Andrew felt a surge of annoyance,

"I..I", he was going to say that he didn't need

her hand-holding at any time, but realised that in fact she was telling the truth, and as the adage had it, truth hurt.

"I didn't mean for support Emily, I meant for company, after all, we are sort of engaged now aren't we?"

"Of course we are Andrew, and I didn't mean it to sound so cruel", brushing her lips across his ear-lobe, she whispered, "you could be more forceful though, couldn't you?"

The touch of her mouth thrilled him but he pulled away and said, "Of course", he could still feel a tingling sensation and rubbed fiercely at his ear as he added, "not now though, I'll be more forceful with you when this lot's settled".

Emily laughed.

"I didn't mean with me, I meant in your attitude with other people".

"And that", Andrew smiled wickedly as they crossed the road to Karim.

"What about the rooms?" called Anderson, "Are you going to take them?"

Emily squeezed Andrew's hand as he gazed at her enquiringly.

"Yes", he shouted, "Keep the rooms, we'll be back".

As they reached the hotch potch of tents and make-shift shelters, Abdullah Karim spoke to them,

"Ah, Mister Craig, could you please come with me the Sheikh wishes to meet you".

Andrew nodded as Emily said,

"Good, we've got to see him anyway, Ben Acate asked us..." she stopped as she saw Abdullah shaking his head, "something wrong?" she asked.

"There is I'm afraid Miss Lang, you see, the Sheikh is old fashioned in his ways. You won't be able to speak to him, it's only the men he wishes to talk to. Mind you", he added brightly, "you are at liberty to sit outside his tent with the other women whilst we talk."

Emily bridled.

"I'm not sitting outside some tent like a..."

"Camp-follower", supplied Andrew.

"Whatever", Emily said, "I'm not just a woman", then she scowled, "What am I saying, just a woman, we're as good as men, equal in fact, in all things, so tell your Sheikh if he wants to speak to Andrew, he speaks to me as well", she stared hard at Andrew, "Agreed?"

"Agreed?" she repeated, then when Andrew still didn't answer, "Right you see your Sheikh. I'll go to the hotel, and I might even be there when you've finished you, your gossiping!".

Andrew couldn't fail to get the implied message contained in her statement and he stopped her as she made to walk off.

"Hold on Emily", then to Abdullah in a strong tone, "Miss Lang is my personal assistant so , we go to the sheikh together or not at all".

"Bravo Andrew", cried Emily as Abdullah considered,

"Very well Mister Craig", he said after his deliberation, "I will make the arrangements", bowing, the Arab went into the tent behind him.

"Here we go then", Andrew took her hand and went to follow Abdullah but they stopped as two other Arabs, brandishing swords, barred their way.

Emily gulped nervously as the steel blades clanged together, but Andrew snapped.

"how dare you, we're official visitors".

He felt a surge of anger as they remained impassive but, before it could manifest into something concrete, Abdullah returned.

 A quiet word in Arabic made the two sentries fall back and Karim beckoned Andrew and Emily into the tent.

"It is customary to prostrate oneself on a first audience, " he whispered, " in your case though a bow will be sufficient, and you Miss Lang, if you would sit behind Mister Craig when he is invited to be seated by the Sheikh".

"I suppose so", she agreed grudgingly, then trailed behind the men as they entered the Sheikh's presence.

A lengthy introduction in Arabic, in which Andrew heard his and Emily's names was followed by the Sheikh waving a hand towards a pile of cushions placed on the carpeted floor. He sat, and Emily, trying to appear nonchalant, although mightily impressed with her surroundings, sat behind.

More talk between the sheikh and Abdullah, then Karim turned to Andrew,

"The Sheikh asks if you will take refreshment?"

"I thought we were here to discuss what's

happening?" said Andrew.

Abdullah nodded.

"Yes, but there are customs to be observed, any guest of the Kohani must be fed, their comforts assured, the dust from their long journey taken from their clothes and then, if there is business to discuss, then it is time".

"But we only came from the factory", Andrew turned to Emily for backing but she only smiled and mouthed,

"Comforts, let's have our comforts".

After food and drink had been brought, Abdullah sat crossed legged in front of Andrew and began to speak,

"We are, as you say in English, in a spot of bother, you see, Mister Craig, when Ben Acate stole the potion, he not only ruined the annual ceremony of the mating of the camels, he also made the Sheikh and his family lose face. Each year, the Sheikh makes the potion, using a formula that has been handed down from his ancestors, but, because of Ben Acate's action he can no longer do this."

"Is this why he's here?" Andrew asked.

"The best person to answer that would be the

Sheikh", said Abdullah. "but I digress. The tribe that you see in this village is the immediate family of the Sheikh and they have come to seek the potion". Andrew started to interrupt again but Emily shushed him into silence. "Your officials", Abdullah continued, "they seek to send the Sheikh and his people back home. Oh, it is true they landed here unlawfully, this the Sheikh knows, and the fact that they must shortly leave, But, Mister Craig, before they go, you must help to apprehend Ben Acate, hand him over to the Sheikh, let the Kohani see publicly that he is punished and perhaps, given time, this whole unhappy incident will be forgotten."

Andrew shot a quick glance at the Sheikh, who had been silently watching, then Abdullah spoke again,

"My own small task in your country is to finalise the take-over of the firm belonging to your Sir Humphrey but that is well in hand".

"I have heard about this take-over", said Andrew, "but Emily and I, well, we came to see your s

Sheikh about Ben Acate, he asked us to

intercede for him, he's sorry".

"Really sorry", echoed Emily.

"And it's not fair to threaten to kill him", stated Andrew.

The Sheikh laughed, and to their surprise said in perfect English,

"Not fair to kill the wretch? Was it fair for him to steal from his own people? Mister Craig, and you Miss Lang, seeing you choose to attend the affairs of men, Ben Acate is a dog, lower than a dog in fact, he deserves to die".

"You speak English sir" Andrew said deferentially.

"When it suits my friend, only when it suits", the Sheikh stood up and said sternly, "Now tell Abdullah where Ben Acate is my men will bring him to me and there is an end to this matter. We leave your country and all will be well".

" Don't tell him Andrew", Emily got to her feet and stared at the Sheikh defiantly, "just because he stole your potion".

The Sheikh sighed.

"you don't understand do you Miss Lang, because of this cur's theft, I can no longer be a leader of the Kohani. My sons and their sons to come will never know the honour of leading our people. I can pass down the formula, I could tell you the secret, but without some of the liquid it is useless. Each year I use the potion in our rituals, and each year I make more, and use it as it's base the residue of that has been used".

"You mean that you need some potion before you can make more?" Emily asked excitedly.

"Exactly", said the Sheikh, "Now if you will excuse me, I have to meet some of your officials at the hotel".

"But I've got some potion", she cried.

Stepping over to her, the Sheikh gripped her arm.

"This is true?" he asked.

She nodded , then freeing her arm from his grasp said,

"Ben Acate saved it for you, this was to be his bargaining point for clemency".

The Sheikh called in Arabic and his two sons entered the tent.

"Tariq, Ali, go to the hotel and tell whoever is in charge that I will attend them after an important council we must hold ourselves"

Abdullah halted them as they made to leave then said to the Sheikh,

"Forgive me exalted one, is this a wise thing to do? Should we not attend their meeting, we cannot afford to antagonise the British Government with this take-over imminent."

"Ach, business", the Sheikh snorted, "this is my brother's forte, should I be held to ransom because of a small firm we wish to buy?"

"With apologies", Abdullah bowed, "Your brother is only concerned for your welfare and to this end he feels that the acquisition of this firm would be beneficial to the future of the Kohani".

The Sheikh decided.

"Very well," he said, "Let us go to the hotel, and you Miss Lang, if you possess the potion as you say, then do not let it out of your hands, for if you do?" he patted her cheek, "Perhaps Mister Craig will have to intercede for you as well as Ben Acate".

"You can't threaten us", said Andrew, but it was a wasted statement, the Sheikh and his two sons had left the tent.

"you really have the potion?" asked Abdullah

quietly.

"Of course", replied Emily.

"I thought it all wasted at the factory", Andrew said.

"You have it with you?" Abdullah breathed the question and smiled, but Emily was careful in her answer.

"It's in a safe place".

"Ah, Miss Lang, play games if you like", Abdullah purred the words, "but it might not pay for you to alienate the Sheikh, it...".

Andrew interjected forcefully,

"Threats? We have rights in this country".

"you misunderstand Mister Craig", Abdullah was apologetic, "what I meant was that your possession of the potion is indeed a powerful aid to your intercession on behalf of Ben Acate".

"So the Sheikh will let him off?" asked Emily.

"With a rebuke" Abdullah laughed, "that is something that can only be discovered in due course".

At that moment an Arab entered the tent, stared curiously at Andrew and Emily, then spoke to Abdullah. He answered in Arabic,

then beckoned for Andrew to follow him.
"Trouble Mister Craig, the Sheikh refuses to discuss any matters with your officials, he is asking for you".

"For me?" Andrew sounded incredulous, but Emily beamed proudly and sighed.

"Oh Andrew".

Crossing to the hotel, they entered and were met by an embarrassed-looking police inspector.

"Are you Craig?" then when Andrew nodded, "they're in there, you must really carry some weight, he won't speak to anyone else".

He opened the door to the lounge and, as they went through, the noise that greeted them was if anything more raucous than in the street outside.

The Sheikh was seated at the table, the two Arabs that had stopped Andrew from going into the tent were standing watchfully behind and Tariq and Ali sat either side of their father. Facing them, at first glance, was what seemed like representatives of every branch of the armed forces, the police, customs, and obvious civil servants, and they were all speaking at once.

"Gentlemen, gentlemen, please", a man , who Andrew recognised as a politician he had often seen on the television, banged heavily on the table calling for order.

The noise abated and the politician beckoned Andrew forward.

"Mister Craig?" he asked politely.

Andrew nodded nervously and turned to look for Emily but she was nowhere to be seen.

Chapter 16

Emily Lang was following the man into the hotel when she saw Doctor Bryant and Peter Winfield.

"Hello", they called.

As the Arabs and Andrew disappeared inside, she waited until they approached.

"What're you doing here?" she asked, "Is Sir Humphrey with you?"

"He's gone", said Winfield, grinning, "gone back to London and apparently he's getting the boot from the company, out on his ear, what about that then?"

"Don't laugh", Bryant admonished, "We could be dismissed as well as old Wonnacott".

"Not to worry", Winfield's eyes were everywhere; "Did you ever see anything like this in your life?"

"It's bedlam", observed Bryant, "We had an awful time getting here".

"And us", Emily said, "Our car's in a field up

the road somewhere".

"What's happening?" asked the Doctor.

Emily told them what little she knew as they listened incredulously.

"And now he's been asked to arrange things with the Sheikh", she finished proudly.

"Good for Andrew", Winfield clapped his hands in mock applause, "I didn't know he could speak Arabic though".

"Psst",

Emily knew it was Ben Acate before she even turned around.

"Psst".

Bryant and Winfield stared open-mouthed as the Arab joined their little group.

"What's this 'psst' routine?" asked Winfield.

"That's something else", said Emily, then quickly explained Ben Acate's plight, "And Andrew and I have promised to help him".

"Yes, but killed?" Bryant said unbelievingly, "People don't get killed for theft, not in this country".

"I suppose it depends on what you're thieving", said Winfield, "what about the crown jewels? Fellow got beheaded for nicking them didn't he?"

"I don't think so", answered Bryant.

"Oh blow the crown jewels", Emily sounded angry, "This is Ben Acate's life we're discussing".

"Talking of Arabs" Bryant said, "Where's that chap you brought down here? I've got a message for him. About the take-over", he added as Emily raised a quizzical eyebrow, "Apparently he's got two days to make an offer to Sir Humphrey".

"He's in the hotel with Andrew, so the Arabs are buying the firm eh? The Sheikh must have plenty of money", she observed.

"No", Ben Acate stated emphatically, "His brother Prince Achmed, he has money, oil money, and power. Abdullah is his servant, the Sheikh is a true Kohani, children of the desert, they need no money".

"So why steal the potion?" Emily shot the question at him, "You tried to get money for that".

"Well", the Arab was evasive, "In England one needs money I could not work", he began to wail and beat his chest, "I have betrayed my tribe, my sheikh..."

"Stop that," said Emily, "I'm already helping so there's no need to get dramatic again".

"Come on Sid", said Winfield, "Let's go in and give this other chap the message eh?"

"Not me", said Emily, "you two can go, I've an idea I want to discuss with Ben Acate", she gripped the Arab's arm, "Besides I don't think he'd be welcome just now".

Bryant and Winfield watched as Emily and the Arab disappeared into the crowd.

"What do you make of that then?" asked Winfield, as he and Bryant went into the hotel.

"Don't rightly know", replied the Doctor, "I don't even begin to understand where they all come from, it's like a Zoo".

"You heard old Wonnacott on the phone didn't you? They must have landed at Tilbury Docks".

"Magic carpet more like" muttered Bryant.

The entrance hall was filled with people, Arabs smilingly nodding to everybody in sight, worried looking men in civilian garb huddled in groups, whispering agitatedly to each other and several members of the armed forces who had apparently been borrowed from Madame

Tussauds, for they had formed a tableau in a corner of the room, unmoving, silent, grim.

"Hello gents", Reg Anderson approached, "Can't do a meal I'm afraid if you've come for lunch".

"Not lunch", Bryant said, "We've come on an errand, where's that Arab bloke, the one staying here with…"

"You must be joking", Anderson laughed, "Arabs? There are millions of them, which one would you like?"

"I don't mean this lot, you know the fellow, he came from the plant this morning with Andrew Craig".

"Oh yes, he's in the lounge with the Sheikh and someone from the home office, there's a hell of a stink on, seems the Arabs landed at a disused airfield just a few miles from here and …"

"I thought they came in at Tilbury?"

"Hell no", Anderson said, "I've been listening and I tell you, it's like a comic opera in there, the army's blasting the air force, the air force is blaming the government, the government's blaming anyone…"

"Yes, all right", Winfield touched Anderson's arm, "Get to more important things, can we at least have a drink?"

"Of course, we've got booze left. Come into the bar". Anderson winked slyly, "you can hear what's going on in there".

The three men went into the bar where Mrs. Anderson served them.

"Stand here", Reg Anderson ushered them along the bar counter to where it curved into the lounge area, then help a finger to his lips, "Listen!"

The politician that Andrew had recognised, who was actually the under-secretary of state for the home office, held the floor.

"And with utmost respect sir", he was saying, "Your action in landing here is at the very least a severe breach of our regulations, and a flagrant disregard of any diplomatic agreement; we have between our two countries".

Tariq, the Sheikh's son spoke in Arabic, as Peter Winfield, who by this time was peeping round the bar partition, whispered a blow by blow account on the proceedings.

The sheikh rose and motioned to Andrew to go

with him as he walked to a quiet corner of the room,

"What is it sir?" asked Andrew.

"Ah Mister Craig, you see before you a man with a heavy heart, I have no stomach for this bickering, your government, they want me to go home and I wish to go home, but Ben Acate, he stole the potion and without that the Kohani are nothing", the Arab chieftain stared out of a nearby window, "look there, Mister Craig, my people followed me to England but they did not want to, the desert is their home and it calls them as it calls me".

Raised voices made him pause and look toward the doorway, someone shouted, a police whistle sounded, then incredibly, the lounge erupted in a mass of struggling men. Suddenly above the din came Emily's cry.

"Andrew!"

Galvanised into immediate action by the sound of her voice, he plunged into the melee.

Peter Winfield fell into the room as he craned his neck too far and overbalanced, and Doctor Bryant, together with Reg Anderson went swiftly to his rescue when it seemed he might be trampled under the feet of the surging crowd.

A chair broke, the snapping of it's legs sharp above the uproar and Anderson blanched, "Mind the furniture", he called, but his voice was lost in the tumult.

Andrew sighted Emily and fought his way to her.

"What happened?" he screamed.

"I don't know" she shouted, and held him tightly, "I brought Ben Acate in here, he took off his hood, then all hell was let loose. Some Arabs grabbed him, the police grabbed the Arabs.." a tear ran down her cheek.

"Never mind love", Andrew started to move, pulling her with him.

"Save me Mister Craig", a dishevelled Ben Acate barred their progress, "You promised..." his words ended in a gurgle as another Arab leapt on his back and dragged him down into the heaving mass of bodies.

"Get him Andrew" Emily howled, "Please, he's got the potion".

"The potion?" Andrew shouted the question as a sudden lull occurred in the fighting and his words echoed about the room.

"The potion, potion", it was taken up and whispered, called, it was spoken loudly, reverently all thoughts of battle were forgotten as around the lounge was repeated these seemingly magic word, "The potion!"

A barked command in Arabic made the tribesmen gather at one end of the lounge where several police officers, decidedly the worse for wear, eyes them balefully.

Other men struggled from the floor as Reg Anderson moved among them, trying desperately to assess the damage that had been caused by the fracas.

"There he is" said Peter Winfield, pointing to Abdullah Karim.

"Oh yes", Sydney Bryant stepped over to him, I've got a message from Sir Humphrey, he says you've got two days to come up with an offer!"

"The take-over?" Abdullah nodded, "Fret not good sir, there are others working for us who will deal with this matter, they are already in London".

"Oh I see", Doctor Bryant came back to Winfield, "Waste of time that Peter, he's not too bothered at all".

"I'm bothered Sid, someone kicked me when I was on the floor, is my drink still on the bar there?"

"Never mind your drink., look what's going on now".

The Sheikh stood in front of a half-circle of Arabs and Ben Acate knelt facing him.

A stream of Arabic came from the kneeling man's lips as he held out a glass bottle.

"That's what I gave Emily Lang", said Winfield, "it's the potion I had left".

"Shush" Bryant nudged him into silence.

The Sheikh spoke, then Tariq, his eldest son took up a position behind Ben Acate and held out an unsheathed knife.

"Now then ,now then" an intrepid police constable stepped forward from the crowd of onlookers, "I thought you lot was told that weapons would be confiscated, hand it over lad, hand it over".

The policeman didn't get near Tariq however for he found his way blocked by a group of Arabs who used their bodies to firmly shepherd him to the side of the room.

More Arabic from the Sheikh as he took the proffered potion, then Abdullah intoned in English,

"Who speaks for Ben Acate".

"Go on Andrew", Emily gave him a slight push in the back and he stepped forward.

"I, er, I wish to speak on his behalf".

The Sheikh rattled off something in his own tongue which made the tribesmen laugh, then in English,

"Don't be embarrassed my friend, I said nothing detrimental to you, my people laugh only because a foreigner defends one of our own wrongdoers".

"Well," began Andrew, "If you could spare Ben Acate!"

"Ah, Mister Craig", the Sheikh interrupted him, "See this?" he led up the potion, "With this liquid I am once again the true ruler of the Kohani. I know that you and your lady gave it to Ben Acate to use as a lever for my forgiveness, but there was no need", he continued, "If you yourself would have handed me this, I would have given you anything".

"So you won't kill him?"

"Kill him? Mister Craig, we are not barbarians", he waved his hand, "Take him, he is yours", he said, "do with the miserable wretch what you will".

At a sign from his father Tariq moved away from Ben Acate and sheathed his blade.

"Do we return home now?" he asked.

The Sheikh nodded.

"The quicker we are home the sooner I can make some of the potion, perhaps even this year's mating ceremony may be saved".

"Ahem", Andrew cleared his throat, "If you want to", he began, "you could possibly use the laboratory at the plant to make your potion. Peter Winfield is the chemist there, he would be only too pleased to help you".

"As splendid idea", the Sheikh slapped him on the back, "let us leave now".

"There is still the matter of returning you all to your own country", the voice came sternly and as Andrew turned he saw the under-secretary standing there. The politician went on, "And seeing, my dear Sheikh that you miraculously learned to speak English in the last half-hour, perhaps we could continue our discussion".

"As Allah wills it" said the Sheikh resignedly, "So shall it be".

Chapter 17

"I'm impressed" said Emily when she and Andrew were on their own.

"What do you mean?" he asked.

"You" , she hugged him, "I'm really impressed".

Andrew flushed.

"Why"? he said, "I've done nothing".

"No?" Emily pointed towards the lounge, What about the people in there eh? You get sent here by Sir Humphrey, cos he thinks you'll do anything for him, and now look at you, in charge of this potion affair, sorting things out for those Arabs and the foreign secretary. Oh yes Andrew , I'm impressed".

"It's the home office", he said, reddening, then when she gazed inquiringly, "the member of parliament, he's from the home office. Under-secretary or something, still", he shrugged, "I suppose I have helped in some way".

Emily laughed.

"Hark at him. Duty hero and blasé to the end

and I thought I knew you".

He smiled self –consciously and squeezed her hand,

"I did what I had to, that's all".

"And what about us?" she asked tenderly, "Was that something you just had to do"?

"When I said that you were my fiancée?" she nodded, then Andrew kissed her, "I meant every word", he breathed.

At that moment Mrs. Anderson came from the kitchen.

"Look at you two", she exclaimed, "Still here? And I bet you haven't had anything to eat have you?"

"Food" Andrew broke from their embrace.

Mrs. Anderson giggled, "If you're hungry, I'm just about to make Reg a bit of tea, and I know he wouldn't mind you joining us.

"A sandwich would be fine Mrs. Anderson wouldn't it Em?"

Emily nodded.

"Yes", I'm starving.

"Starving?" Reg Anderson's voice heralded his arrival from the bar, "come and have a drink, there's plenty of nuts and things in here".

"Reg" his wife spoke sternly, "they're eating with us upstairs, and don't talk about drinking, you sound as if you've had more than enough".

"Only a few snorts with my friends love, that's all", he called behind him, "come and meet the wife gents".

"A pleasure Ma'am" a be-medalled Air-Force officer emerged from the bar followed by an Army Captain and Police Constable Charles Emery.

"Did I hear you mention grub Mrs. A" asked the P.C.

"Food, eh", the army officer spoke, "I wouldn't say no to a swift bite".

"And who's going to bite you", Anderson asked, then collapsed into fits of laughter as the others looked on in amazement.

"Dashed clever turn of wit your husband's got" commented the R.A.F man.

Charlie emery stepped closer to the good lady.

"If you was making something Mrs. A?"

Mrs. Anderson dithered for a moment then making a decision, said,

"all right, if you've finished trying to drink the

bar dry, follow me, I'll fix something for everyone".

They all trooped upstairs after Mrs. Anderson , Reg trailing behind carrying a nearly full bottle of whiskey.

After eating, five people sat around the dining table and , figuratively at least, belched.

"Empty your cups", Reg instructed, "We'll have a drop of the hard stuff to finish".

Just then there was a knock at the door and a uniformed police inspector came in.

"sorry to disturb you", he said, "Mister Craig and wing-commander Ellis?"

"Have a drink" said Reg Anderson still trying to force his whiskey on anyone who would show an interest.

Andrew stood up as the Air-force man said, "I'm Ellis old boy, what's up?"

"If you and Mister Craig could accompany me..."

"To the station," cried Anderson, "I've seen that on the films, they always say that, " he cackled drunkenly as the others stared.

"shush Reg", admonished his wife, "you're making a right show of yourself".

"It's true" he claimed then turning to P.C. Emery, "tell them Charlie, you're a copper, tell them it's true".

Charlie remained seated then jumped to his feet as the inspector barked,

"Are you on duty Constable?"

"No, er, no sir" Emery faltered, then, "relieved sir, the doctor relieved me from duty, I had a shock when I saw those Arabs sir".

"You're relieved?" the inspector said, "Not as relieved as I am though. Shall we go gentlemen?"

"Wait for me", cried Emily as the air-force man and Andrew followed the policeman from the room "thanks again Mrs. Anderson that was lovely".

"Welcome you are my dear, welcome", her words trailed Emily as she left the room on the heels of the three men.

As they entered the lounge, Andrew noticed that the Sheikh had gone, but Abdullah Karim was sitting facing the Under-Secretary. He smiled a greeting as Andrew approached and the politician spoke.

"Ah, Mister Craig, and you must be Squadron

Leader Ellis?"

"Yes sir", the officer replied, "But it's Wing Commander actually".

"Well sit yourselves down and tell me about these Arab chaps landing".

"Ahem", the police officer cleared his throat, "We have the crews detained at the airfield sir".

"The crews?", how many planes are there? And more importantly, how on earth did they get past our air defences, don't we have radar in the South-East?"

"Twenty men in all sir", the inspector began but lapsed into silence as Ellis started to speak,

"They were picked up on our radar sir. Five planes, Hercules military transports. They were challenged then escorted down by fighter wing. Normal routine sir".

"Don't tell me that Wing-Commander. I've just spent the past few hours arguing that very point with your superiors. This is far from being 'normal', as you put it", he paused, then, "what baffles me is that a tribe of Arabs can land in our country and go on their merry way carte-blanche. It doesn't say a lot for our security does it?"

"The Army was informed sir", the inspector said, "We passed the responsibility.."

Stupid man". The politician snapped, "Responsibility? In all matters of national security responsibility remains with everyone. Now", he looked at Ellis, "What about these aircraft?"

"Hercules, sir, five of them, they're a turbo-prop job, fly at roughly thirty to thirty five thousand feet . Their capacity is such that they could easily carry all your Arabs, their animals and probably a lot more".

"Mm, I see", said the M.P. "So what they could carry here they could conceivably carry back again?"

"Piece of cake sir", Ellis smiled, "They're a short take-off craft and not only could they land where they did but at.." he began to list airfields but the politician interrupted him.

"Spare me the gazetteer, I'm only interested in their ability to go back where they've come from. What about fuel?"

"The tanks they're fitted with could easily bring them from Africa sir".

"That's not what I asked wing-Commander, what about getting these people home?"

"Well, sir, given a range of...".

"Don't waffle", the under-secretary banged the arm of his chair, "A plain yes or no, that's all I want, can we re-fuel them where they are?..And can they fly home?"

"Yes sir!".

"Right! Then this is how the Prime Minister wants the situation resolved. Abdullah Karim, you and your two companions will return to normal airlines, you have passports?" the Arab nodded, "The bulk of the tribe will prepare to leave the village in the morning. They will be escorted by army units to the airfield where they will embark and take off when your people say they can do so", this to wing-commander Ellis and when he nodded, "The planes will be re-fuelled tonight you?" another bob of the head, "Then gentlemen, let's sincerely hope that this is an end to a regrettable incident".

"What about me", said Andrew, "Do I do anything?"

"No mister Craig", the politician smiled, "We appreciate the help you have given us, but from now on the matter is in the hands of the armed forces".

Wing-commander Ellis stood and saluted as the under-secretary rose from his chair.

"If there is nothing else gentlemen", no one spoke, "then let us call everyone back in and we'll finalise the details".

Andrew turned quickly away to hide his grin, as Emily began to hum the 'Dam buster's march".

"So that appears to be that Mister Craig" Andrew turned as Abdullah Karim spoke, and stood arm in arm with Emily as he replied, "Yes it does rather, so could you possibly tell us where we stand?"

"Stand?" the Arab sounded puzzled.

"I think Andrew means about our jobs" Emily supplied, "Do we go back to London? Have we been sacked or what?"

"But you are here", said Abdullah, "In charge at the factory. Yes?"

"While the potion was being analysed" Andrew stated, "But now, well, the firm's being taken over isn't it?"

"Possibly Mister Craig", Abdullah said, "I personally have made some representation to that end but we have an English firm in our organisation who have been doing the groundwork for some time now", he looked towards the street, "when I have informed the Sheikh of your governments arrangements to get my people home I will contact London and find out what is happening".

The Arab waved a hand as Emily thanked him, then left the hotel.

"What now?" Andrew asked Emily.

She whispered in his ear,

"What did you say?"

"I'd like to..." she didn't have to finish the words.

"N...now?" he stuttered, then as she nodded,

"But where?" he asked, fighting to control his emotions.

She pointed at the upper floor.

"Oh yes." Andrew clutched her hand, "Where the Arabs were staying", he almost dragged her to the stairs and they began to climb them two at a time.

Reaching the corridor, he waited no longer and, seizing Emily, pressed his lips to hers, then, in a passionate embrace, they sidled crab-fashion across the carpeted floor, kissing, touching, his eager mouth drinking deeply of hers, then kissing her hair, her neck, the blistering heat of their need threatening to engulf them both.

"Oh Andrew", she breathed.

"Oh God", he groaned, then turning the handle of the bedroom door, pulled her inside and slammed the portal closed with an almighty crash.

Quickly they reached for each other and clung together fiercely as Andrew fumbled desperately at her clothing.

"I can help Mister Craig sir".

The couple sprang apart, startled.

"What?" Andrew's face was scarlet as he stared at the speaker, Ben Acate, he snarled, "What are you doing here?"

"It is our room honoured sir" the Arab salaamed, "I am here to serve you".

Emily straightened her dress as Andrew spluttered, "What do you mean serve me? Get out, get out now and stay out".

"But my master gave me to you sir", Ben Acate said in some bewilderment, "you saved my life and now that worthless life is yours, to do with what you will".

"Do with him what you will", the Sheikh's words echoed in Andrew's brain.

"I don't want your life" he persisted, "Go away".

"I have been waiting your commands sir", the Arab ignored his plea as he moved to the bed, "Shall I prepare this for you sir?"

Andrew Craig glared.

"No", he shouted, then catching Emily's hand, "come on, if he won't go we will".

In the corridor, Andrew leaned against the wall and took a deep breath, then producing his inhaler, went to use it.

"Never", said Emily surprisingly, "Still got that? Thought you'd finished with it ages ago".

He stared at the inhaler, breathed tentatively, then replaced it in his pocket.

"Funny, I haven't used it have I?"

Emily shook her head.

"Nor your glasses", she commented, "And the limp?" smilingly she added, "It's got to be a minor miracle hasn't it?"

"Then it's you who's performed it" he said softly and reached for her.

"Oh no", Emily backed away, "Not with Ben Acate the other side of that door" she planted a swift kiss on his cheek, "Forgive me Andrew, I couldn't".

"I know what you mean" he agreed reluctantly, "Let's go downstairs, I'll see that Sheikh, tell him to have the man back again, I certainly don't want him".

Together, they went downstairs and left the hotel in search of the leader of the Kohani.

Tom Allenby allowed himself a satisfied smile as he replaced the telephone receiver.

The calls he'd made to the major share-holders of Farm Chemicals, and the assurances he's received guaranteed there would be no hitch at the vote would be for acceptance of the take-over and, without Sir Humphrey Wonnacott, there would be no change of heart.

He looked around his office, true, he'd come up in the world in a very short time, but he wasn't finished yet, not by a long way. Just think, started as a salesman, then on the board, and now M.D., managing director, what next? 'Chairman', he said the word aloud. It was thanks to the chairman that he'd moved up so fast. Perhaps the old boy had recognised a kindred spirit, Tom chuckled, then thinking of Sir Humphrey, his face became serious and once again he went over what had happened. Since the company had started to go downhill, tom had constantly been on the look-out for something else, something beneficial to himself of course, and this imminent take-over appeared to be going to benefit him no matter what way it turned out. Mind you, a couple of large firms had lost interest and the Arabs hadn't come back with an offer, but Cott Industries had, and with the money already deposited against the agreed share price there was no former offer than that.

Tom debated whether to call the company secretary again but decided against the action, it would be giving in to his fears that something might go wrong even at this late stage. But, what could go wrong? His own shares had been forfeited for a stake in the new company, Cott Industries Limited. That had been an inspired move, a move that Sir Humphrey himself would have approved of, well, he used to have a reputation for wheeling and dealing, but now the poor chap must be getting old, allowing his control to slip, being put out to grass with what on the surface was a handsome pay-out but, what he'd finish up with probably wouldn't keep him in cigars.

No sympathy though, the King was dead, long live the King, and that could be me, tom thought.

Closing the file on his desk, he placed it in the drawer, locked it, then standing up, went out into the corridor.

Then he stopped. Light from the half-open door of the chairman's sanctum streamed across the floor.

Tom Allenby looked at his watch then furtively, he moved until he could see around the corner of the door-frame.

Sir Humphrey Wonnacott sprawled in his padded chair, feet resting on his desk. Smoke from a cigar clenched firmly in his mouth curled lazily upward and Tom saw he held an almost full goblet of brandy.

"You're late aren't you", Tom pushed open the door and moved into the room.

"Hello Tom", cried the chairman as he removed the cigar from his mouth, "Yes, I am pretty late, what about you? Burning the midnight oil?".

"I'm on my way home", declared Allenby, "I've been tying up some loose ends for the meeting tomorrow".

"The board meeting", then as tom nodded, "And I suppose it's off with the old and on with the new eh? Well, I'll drink to that, join me?"

"I will. Just one though" Tom sat and watched as Sir Humphrey brought the decanter and another glass from the cabinet.

"Might as well keep it handy", remarked Humphrey as he poured a generous measure in Tom's glass then sat down again, "Cheers".

"Cheers Humphrey!" Tom drank then, feeling some sort of pity, compassion or just a guilty conscience, said quietly,

"I am sorry you know".

"Sorry, for what?"

"You know the way things have turned out, Farm Chemicals coming to the end of the road, you leaving".

"Oh yes, me leaving", the chairman studied Tom, "and what about you tom. You're staying with the new people I hear".

"How...?" Allenby was taken by surprise, then recovering his composure, "I don't know how you knew, but what else could I do? I can't go anywhere and have the position I've got here".

"You're staying though Tom", the chairman was persistent, "Made a deal haven't you?"

"I think so", Tom replied calmly, but inside he was desperately trying to think who could have told the chairman of his scheme, "It's a job though, only a job".

"Worth your while is it?" Wonnacott seemed to be enjoying Tom Allenby's discomfort.

"Don't know yet" tom sought to change the subject, "Pity we didn't get a result from the potion or the Arabs".

"Mmm", Sir Humphrey was non-committal, "you'll be signing Farm chemicals away Tom?"

"No", tom started to explain, "According to the Board of Trade people, the share-holders deal with their own stock and transference is on the actual receipt of their stock certificates, the firm itself..." he paused. "Why am I telling you this, you know more about the routine than I'll ever know. Besides the actual papers will have to be signed by you, that's why you must be at the meeting", he leaned forward, "You've got to meet the Cottage Industries people anyway, there's lots for you to do."

"It's Cott industries Tom".

"Cott then, you've still got to be there".

Sir Humphrey refilled both glasses, ignoring the shaking of Tom's head.

"It won't hurt you Tom, drink it".

The chairman obeyed his own words by swallowing a good measure of the fiery spirit then said,

"I told you before Tom, no way will I put myself in the position of a naughty boy having his wrist slapped so, after you phoned Simon Ericson..."

"How, how did you know that?" gasped Tom, Ericson was their biggest share-holder, a Vice-chairman of his own company who stayed out of the public eye at his own request.

"I rang him just after you did, asked if he'd received my letter of resignation".

Tom's eyes widened, he gulped his brandy, coughed, then, with tears streaming down his face croaked,

"Resignation, you, resigned?" You can't",

He subsided in a fit of coughing.

Sir Humphrey laughed heartily, got up from his chair and moved round the desk to slap tom on the back.

"Don't choke yourself on my behalf Tom", he sat down again, "Of course I can resign, I've just done so".

"That means, er", Tom sought for words, "What's, well, are you going?"

"Now? At this moment?" Sir Humphrey beamed at his hapless protégé, "Leave my lovely office?"

"Course not, course not", Tom said swiftly, but not as swiftly as his mind was working. This was a turn up for the books and no mistake.

"There's things for you to do though, you must have stuff to take away". He stopped and stared at Sir Humphrey who was shaking with suppressed laughter. Immediately Tom felt a sinking feeling in the pit of his stomach, something had gone wrong, the chairman was too happy. He stood up slowly.

"Humphrey, why are you laughing?"

"It's you Tom, so full of yourself you've missed out on what's happening around you".

"What do you mean?"

"Have you only had eyes for yourself? Haven't you read the memo that's been going the rounds, the article in F.T.?"

"I don't know what you are going on about Humphrey", Tom sat down and gripped his brandy glass as he stared at the chairman.

"Look at you" Sir Humphrey exclaimed, "Blabbing on about Cottage industries. It's Cott Industries Tom, Cott…as in Wonnacott, I'm Cot Industries".

"You can't be", Tom Allenby gulped his drink then wheezed, "You're not allowed to buy your own firm, you've got a vested interest, it's insider trading, you…"

"Don't talk such drivel Tom", the chairman became serious, "I've just told you, I resigned from Farm Chemicals as soon as the take-over became imminent, and as for buying it, as you rightly said old friend, I am personally broke, and the office cat has more shares in the company than I've got, so," he began to smile again, "Cott industries is bidding on behalf of the Arabs".

"But you can't" Tom Allenby's voice was despairing, "the Arabs never got back to us, they made no offer".

"Yes" Sir Humphrey began to explain, "That was the part that bothered me, then I cast about and came up with all sorts of information. You see Tom, that Abdullah Karim is no more than a servant, well, a high-powered one at that, but he works for a prince, Achmed by name, the brother of that fellow who turned up at Whitley Warren with his tribe. Are you following me?" he gave a little chuckle as he stared at Allenby's face, Tom looked sick.

"Just like the Arabian Nights isn't it? Anyway you'll be pleased to know that the idea of me leaving the firm is still on. The o only thing is", he paused, "Farm Chemicals will still exist, up in Swansea they'll be. Here, this is to be the headquarters of a new company, and guess what?" Once again he stopped, but Tom didn't attempt to speak, he couldn't, "I'm to be the chairman", Sir Humphrey finished.

"How did you?" Tom started to speak, then drank some brandy, "I don't understand", he started again, "How could you be Cott Industries when you were still chairman?" there was no reply, "And how could you strike bargains with this prince, this Achmed, you didn't even know him".

"Don't strain your brain working it out Tom", the chairman deigned to answer, "Just try to remember what I told you when you said we were going to the dogs, I might now know anything about phosphates, but I do know money, and people who know me know that, so, when out of town folk need someone to act on their behalf, who gets recommended?"

Tom Allenby nodded slowly.

"I suppose that's it for me now, the end", he sighed, "as soon as everything is finalised, you shall have my resignation".

"Utter nonsense", the chairman snorted, "Accept your resignation? Ha", he smiled wickedly, "I want you in the new firm Tom, nice and handy to keep my eye on you, besides, you can keep me on my toes, I was getting a bit lazy".

Tom thought for a moment, could he stand it with Sir Humphrey breathing down his neck? But wasn't he doing that now?

"I'd be happy to have the opportunity to continue working with you", he smiled.

The brandy decanter was tipped over both glasses as the office filled with the chairman's hearty laughter.

Chapter 18

Abdullah Karim came over as Andrew and Emily emerged from the hotel.

"Good news my friends, the Kohani return home".

"I know", said Andrew, "I was there remember?"

"Of course", Abdullah nodded, "But now, my people are striking their tents", it was a superfluous statement for they could see the activity where billowing canvas was being pulled and folded into packs small enough to sling on the backs of some patient animals that stood waiting.

"I need to see the Sheikh", Andrew said, "It's Ben Acate, he's..."

"Shortly Mister Craig, he has told me of your offer".

"What offer?"

"To use the facilities of your factory to make the potion",

"Oh that", Andrew smiled ruefully, "You'll have

to see Doctor Bryant, I haven't asked him yet".
"But you are the man who has helped us. The Sheikh trusts you".
Andrew stared at him, bemused,
"Do you know", he began, "I don't believe any of this is happening, I haven't done anything, yet everyone regards me as some sort of golden boy", he turned to Emily, "Tell him love", then as he saw the expression on her face, "No, don't bother, you're the same as this lot".
She didn't utter a word, but the way she squeezed his hand spoke volumes.
Abdullah gave a huge grin.
"Mister Craig, it is possibly the English way to be so modest, but some men are chosen by Allah for his own purposes, and you are such a man, a gifted one".
"I have no gifts", protested Andrew, "I'm an ordinary accountant who's been thrown into the middle of God knows what".
"Exactly Mister Craig, God does know what, so why not return to the hotel, wait for the Sheikh, help with his task and then go forward, together with this lovely lady and fulfil your destiny", the Arab bowed and touched his

forehead before striding off towards the tents.
"Wasn't that lovely Andrew?" Emily sighed, "It is our destiny isn't it?"
"What is? Our intention to get married?" He shook his head, "We'll need some money first, what if we lose our jobs?"
Emily gave him a hard look. Andrew was certainly no romantic.
"Yes dear" she said, "Come on let's find Mrs. Anderson and see if we can get a cup of tea". Threading their way through the crush of people in the entrance hall, Andrew and Emily went into the bar.
"Hello, you two" Reg Anderson greeted them as he leaned on the polished surface of the counter nursing an extremely large whiskey.
"Welcome to this haven from the maddening crowd", he said, waving his glass, "Fancy a drink?"
"Not me", Emily shuddered, "You Andrew?" he shook his head as she continued, "What we would like is a nice cup of tea".
"Nip upstairs", Reg said, "the wife's pouring black coffee down some army bloke's throat, he was out to the world on our settee", he waved a

hand to the bottles arrayed behind the bar, "Come and have a proper drink later, hurry though, there's not a lot left".

"No thanks", said Emily, "we'll settle for tea". She and Andrew went from the bar and pushed their way through what seemed to be an increasing mass of uniformed figures, to the foot of the door.

"Never mind the tea", Andrew muttered quickly, then as Emily stared questioningly, "There's Ben Acate by the door"

"So", then seeing Andrew's expectant look, she smiled knowingly and together, they ran lightly up the stairs and along to the room they had vacated earlier.

Entering, Andrew clasped her in his arms and raised his lips to hers in a soft but demanding kiss.

"Oh love", Emily murmured, then skittishly, "Now what?"

She shivered expectantly as he stared at her with smouldering eyes; emotions ran amok through her tingling frame.

"First things first", he whispered as he released her from his embrace, then slowly, deliberately, he shot the bolt on the bedroom door.

A knocking at the door of the room roused Andrew from a deep sleep. For one brief moment he lay in a limbo of unawareness, not knowing where he was or what had awoken him. Then, he stretched and as his searching fingers touched he softness of Emily's hair, realisation flooded his being.
The noise continued as he gently shook her from her slumber.
"Mmm", she purred, and smiled up into his eyes as he leaned over her, "Come here", her arms snaked lazily from the cocoon of the bedding and pulled him down onto the warm nest of her bosom. The beating of her heart throbbed in his ear and he felt such a wave of desire that he trembled violently, then in a muffled whisper said,
"There's someone knocking".
"Let them", she murmured, her lips brushing his tantalisingly, then caressing his face, his neck.

He groaned, enjoying to the full the delicious sensations coursing through his body then turned on his back as she moved sinuously on top of him.

"Emillleee" the syllables of the word dragged out in a heartfelt entreaty as she began a slow writhing motion.

"Mister Craig" the knocking was repeated as they both heard his name shouted, again it came, Emily rolled off and threw her arms wide.

"I suppose you'd better answer."

Andrew got up and hastily pulled on his shirt and trousers, then going to the door, he called "Who is it, who's there?"

"Abdullah Karim, Mister Craig, the Sheikh would see you".

Andrew turned, Emily was standing at the side of the bed and for a moment he admired her statuesque nakedness.

"What shall we do?" the question caught in his throat and emerged as a strangled croak.

Emily grinned.

"Tell him you'll be there in a few minutes" she began to gather her scattered clothing, "I want the bathroom".

Deciding on his action, Andrew called through the door, "I'll be there in a few minutes".

"In the lounge Mister Craig" the voice faded as Abdullah went away.

"What time is it?" asked Emily.

"My watch!" he crossed to the small table by the window, "Cor, look at this", he said as he gazed down the street.

It was as bright as day below, with two mobile searchlights that had obviously been brought to illuminate the camp-site.

"Watch" said Emily.

"I am", remarked Andrew as he took in the feverish activity around the Arab encampment, "They've packed all the tents now", he commented, "That's from this afternoon when we saw them loading those camels".

"Watch", Emily reached across and picked up his wrist-watch from the table.

"Oh" he said , realising what she had been saying, then as she held it up for him to see, "Just gone six", he made a rapid calculation, "that means it's tomorrow. We've been here all night".

Emily nodded.

It was more like a quarter of an hour before Andrew found himself at the door of the lounge but he hesitated with his hand on the handle as he heard raised voices inside. Glancing round the entrance hall, which was deserted, he walked through the bar area and stood listening before going into the lounge.

"No", the fierceness of the sound made even Andrew flinch and he stepped to where he could see who was talking. The Sheikh, together with Abdullah Karim was sitting with the official from the Home Office.

"No, no, no", the under-secretary thundered, his face red with suppressed anger. Andrew moved further into the room but his presence was ignored.

The politician pointed a trembling finger, "If I allow you to leave, then everyone will want to".

"Forgive me" the Sheikh said patiently, "but is it not true that we travel today"?

"Yes, it is true", the Home Office man replied, "But it will be a controlled exodus, not go when you feel like it".

The Sheikh turned to Abdullah, spoke rapidly in Arabic, waved a hand towards the Under-secretary, then leaning back in his chair said, "Please conduct any further conversation with Karim, your arguments are straining my limited knowledge of the English language."

"There is no argument", stated the official, "I say that you cannot leave the village until you are escorted to the airfield for your journey home".

"Sir", Abdullah was smiling, "The Said is aware of the need for him to leave this country with his people and is full of regret for the inconvenience he has caused you and your government, but he is only desirous of visiting the factory at the invitation of Mister Craig, who has kindly offered the use of the laboratory there so the Sheikh can make some potion to go home with. It's a matter of face you understand?"

"I understand" the official replied "And the answer is still no". He paused, then, "you go with Mister Craig, we have no objection to that".

Abdullah spoke in Arabic to the Sheikh, they

laughed, then Karim turned back and said, "Alas, although I am Kohani, the secret of the potion lies only with the Sheikh".

"His sons?"

"They went with an advance party to the airfield."

"On who's authority?" the Home office representative snapped the question, then when there was no reply, "Right, I'll see about this", he rose to his feet. "As soon as I hear that the aircraft are ready, then the army will escort you and your people out".

The Sheikh sat expressionless as the official stalked from the room.

"He seems to be upset" ventured Andrew.

"Ah, Mister Craig" said the Sheikh, "Have you a car?"

"Yes, but not here, the army took it, I don't drive anyway, Emily…".

Abdullah muttered something to the Sheikh.

"I see", the Sheikh nodded.

At that moment Emily came into the room, "Good morning", she said brightly, "Mrs Anderson is laying on a breakfast of sorts in the dining room".

"No time for that", said the Sheikh, "you are the one that drives?"

"Eh", she flashed a puzzled glance at Andrew,

"The car", he said.

"The car?" she shrugged, "It must still be in that field where the army blokes put it, I haven't even seen the keys yet".

The Sheikh rattled off a phrase in Arabic, then walked out of the room muttering,

"Allah will witness that I am a patient man".

"What's wrong", asked Andrew.

"Well", Abdullah said, "He is what you call in English, frustrated. You must remember that in our country his word is all powerful and he is not used to his wished being thwarted".

"So what now?" Andrew sounded perplexed.

"Breakfast", said Emily firmly.

The Arab nodded.

"That would seem to be the thing to do", he said, " I will go to the Sheikh, find his plans and tell you a little later."

Abdullah walked out with Andrew and Emily and then left them to go to the dining room as he went from the hotel.

Winfield"

"Oh that was good of you" Bryant said sarcastically.

"That's all right", Gates replied, unabashed, "I've been peddling round telling our people to go to work".

"At this hour, but it's still dark" Bryant said , "Anyway, I know you're the shop steward, but you're taking a lot on yourself aren't you? Is Peter going in?"

"I've told him".

"What about Craig and Miss Lang?"

"They're at the hotel, I haven't been in there, only talking to the Arab outside".

"All right, I'll get dressed and be there shortly". Eddy nodded, sat astride his ramshackle machine and made a wavering exit along the drive and out into the street.

"Toast is a breakfast", said Andrew as he bit hungrily into his fourth slice.

"Not much of one", replied Emily, "You should have had an egg or something".

"Got none my love", Mrs. Anderson bustled up

with a large teapot, "Plenty of tea though, refill?"

Andrew nodded and as Mrs. Anderson obliged she carried on speaking, "most of the food's gone now".

"Isn't there a shop in the village?" Emily asked.

"Bless you, yes, of course there's a shop, but what with these Arabs, and the villagers not being able to go anywhere, their stock didn't last five minutes. Still.." she moved away saying, "won't be long now , all back to normal".

"What's normal" thought Andrew as he watched her stepping around the tables in the dining room, filling the proffered cups for the few people that still remained in the hotel. Suddenly, a shrill ululation sounded from outside and startled, Andrew and Emily joined the rush to the window to see what had caused the noise.

The sky had lightened now and the searchlights stood dark. Two lines of black-clad women banging what looked like tambourines and making that incomparable din, flanked a procession of Bedouin, led by the Sheikh an Abdullah Karim, that moved slowly toward the richly decorated carriage that had brought the Said to the village. Animals were being gathered together, horses saddled, sheep and goats tied to the backs of wagons that even now were starting to move with a clattering and a clanking that brought lights on in all the houses, and made a cacophonous contribution to the guttural exhortations of the Arab herdsmen.

"They're leaving"

The statement was took up and repeated. Several of the army officers took hasty gulps of their tea-cups and went swiftly outside to where squads of soldiers and police constables milled in confused disarray.

"The Home Office official could be seen darting hither and thither, his poise and diplomatic aplomb shattered by the uproarious melee.

"Not much organisation there".

Andrew turned and saw Reg Anderson.

"I thought they were going about ten-o-clock?" he observed.

"They were", Reg chuckled, "That Home Office fellow is doing his proverbial nut. Nobody knows what's happening".

"Psst".

Not again, Andrew stared at Ben Acate, "where have you come from?"

"Please", the Arab bent and whispered in Andrew's ear, "The Sheikh awaits you in the lane!"

"Eh", Andrew looked out of the window, then back at Ben Acate, "the Sheikh is getting in that coach there."

"Shush", the Arab exhorted, then pulling Andrew to one side said, "That is not he, it is one of the Kohani, the sheikh is waiting in the lane".

"And me?" asked Emily as she overheard the Arab's words.

"No fair lady" smiled Ben Acate, "but if you could bring your car to the factory".

"I have no keys".

"Keys" Reg Anderson chipped in, "There's a load of keys on the reception counter, I haven't sorted them yet".

"Mister Craig, please." Ben Acate started to pull him away, Emily caught his other arm, and Reg Anderson moved in time as they made a shuffling progress for a few paces.

"This is ludicrous" Andrew said at last, stopping dead and making the others stop as well. He disentangled his arms, then said to Emily, "I'd better go eh?"She nodded, and he gave her a swift peck on the cheek, "You'll bring the car?"

For her answer she placed her hands on either side of his face and planted a lingering kiss full on his lips.

"Mister Craig" the Arab beseeched him and tugged again at his sleeve.

Reluctantly Andrew pulled away, the taste of Emily hot on his mouth, gave a sigh, then followed the Arab from the room.

Going into the lane, Andrew was surprised to find the Sheikh sitting astride a camel while two others lay patiently on the tarmac.

"Get on" said the Sheikh, "We haven't much time".

Andrew stared at the beast nearest to him and the animal stared back with an unnerving expression on it's face.

"Quickly I say" the Sheikh motioned with a whip, "It cannot hurt you".

Andrew threw his leg across the wooden-framed saddle then held on for dear life as the camel uttered a belching roar and lurched to it's feet.

"Oh my God "he murmured a prayer of supplication as his mount settled to a rolling gait in the wake of the Sheikh's camel.

"Ouch" he yelled, and pulled his leg sharp away as Ben Acate came abreast of him and allowed his own animal to nuzzle at Andrew's foot, "He's bit me" Andrew cried.

"It is a she Mister Craig, it will do you no harm".

Andrew didn't answer, the sudden movement of his leg unbalanced him and he felt himself sliding to one side. Reaching out , he grabbed a handful of coarse hair and shuddered as it came away in his fist."Ugh" he frantically scrubbed his hand across the saddle then clung desperately to the wooden cross-piece to try and stop himself from falling altogether.

Try as he might, he couldn't stay upright and once again his body swung over and his head swayed close to Ben Acate's camel which immediately coughed and sprayed his cheek with moisture.

He pulled himself upright and snatched a handkerchief from his pocket but dropped it without wiping his face as the camel began to pick up speed, making him grab for the saddle again in an effort to stay on it's back.

The motion of the camel now started a nauseous feeling in his stomach and Andrew began to regret eating that fourth slice of toast. By now, they were out on the road and had left the last of the cottages behind.

"Grip with your legs Mister Craig", Ben Acate flashed his teeth at Andrew in a mocking smile, "Go with the motion".

Andrew only uttered a despairing groan in answer as his neck whipped forward, then viciously back, and his body wanted to go sideways.

Suddenly the Sheikh shouted and was answered by a yelled curse, a crashing noise and the tinkling of a bell and , as Andrew followed the leading camel, his eyes took in the sight of an exceedingly bent bicycle lying in the hedge and petrified Eddy Gates cowering away from the passing dun-coloured creatures.

For a moment Andrew felt a tinge of sympathy, but another swaying lurch from the animal beneath him brought him back to the reality of his own precarious position, and he again concentrated on staying mounted.

The ride was an absolute nightmare and when they eventually loped through the gates of the Farm Chemical's plant, it was several moments before Andrew realised they had stopped. Almost retching, he saw through bleary eyes the Sheikh dismount and come over to him.

"Well done Mister Craig, am experience is it not?"

"Get me off please", Andrew's voice was a plaintive bleat.

Ben Acate, also afoot, tapped the camel's front legs with a thin cane. The beast roared as it sank forward on it's knees, and Andrew, forcing his nerveless fingers to let go of the wooden saddle, fell exhausted to the ground. Embarrassed, he scrambled to his feet only to collapse again as his legs refused to hold his weight, "I can't walk", he cried.

"Nonsense" said the Sheikh, "The circulation will return in a moment" he turned to Ben

Acate, "Help him" he ordered.

Supported by the Arab, Andrew led the way to the laboratory where they found Peter Winfield. "Thank the lord, someone's turned up", he grinned, "I thought I was going to be the only one here this morning".

Chapter 19

Emily Lang was sorting through the car keys on the reception desk when Abdullah Karim walked over to her.

"You are driving to the factory?"

"If I can find...." She picked up a labelled bunch, "Here they are", she grinned at the Arab, "now I'm driving to the factory, do you want a lift?"

"If that is possible, and if I might encroach further on your generosity".

"Well?"

"The Sheikh will have to be taken to the airfield On completion of his task".

"That won't be necessary".

They turned to see the under-secretary glaring at Abdullah.

"How long did you think such a ridiculous subterfuge would last?" the official asked.

Abdullah raised his hands expressively as the man continued,

"Stupid, the Sheikh slipping away like that, absolutely stupid. Now I have to send a police car to the factory and have him taken to the airfield under escort". He shook an admonishing finger, "Most of your people have gone on, and it's a damn good job the army was in position otherwise there could have been Arabs and animals all over the countryside", his voice rose, "Do you realise that? There would have been hell to pay".
"And would there not be more hell if it was known that the Sheikh of all the Kohani was taken like a criminal and in chains escorted from your supposedly democratic country?"
"Who mentioned chains?"
"Figuratively speaking of course, and worry not, no doubt when next the O.P.E.C representatives meet, the Sheikh's brother, Prince Achmed Yussuf will not allow such an incident as this to sway his judgment when it comes to vote on oil prices".
The Home Office man stared speculatively at Abdullah and then strode to the doorway and looked out onto the street. Returning, he said quietly,

"The village is clear now", he glanced at his wrist-watch, "I estimate that the Arabs will reach the landing field in about two hours, and a further hour should see them embarked, ready for take-off", he took a deep breath, then."I want the Sheikh there within those two hours", he stated, "And I make it your responsibility to see that he gets there".
Abdullah nodded.
"Its shall be so", he intoned, "And allow me to thank you for your understanding".
As they walked to the car, Emily said, "Blackmail?" Abdullah showed his teeth in a wicked smile, "I merely state facts, Miss Lang, the Prince Achmed does sit with the O.P.E.C. people".
They walked on then,
"I expect to hear from London today", Abdullah said.
"Yes?"
"To confirm that we are the new owners of your factory here".
"It's not my factory", Emily glanced sideways at him, "I asked before, how will that affect our jobs here?"

He countered her question with one of his own, "Your Andrew Craig, he is a good man?"

"We are to be married", Emily replied simply, "Why?"

The Arab merely gave her an enigmatic glance and they got in the car and drove to the plant in comparative silence.

On arriving, they saw Eddy Gates standing nervously by three grazing camels, and as they got out of the car, he said,

"Miss Lang, if you're going in, could you tell Doctor Bryant, I'm not supposed to be looking after animals, I'm the shop steward".

"He's here?" she asked.

"Yes, he gave me a lift, these things knocked me off my bike".

Emily and Abdullah hurried into the building, "I'll got up to Doctor Bryant's office", she said, "You got to the laboratory, that door there", then as Abdullah hesitated, "Yes that's the one, go in".

She ran lightly up the stairs as she heard the Sheikh and Peter Winfield speaking to Karim. Opening the door to Bryant's office, she went in and found Andrew and the Doctor drinking the seemingly everlasting coffee that appeared to be the staple diet in the good doctor's room.

"Heard the news?" asked Bryant as she entered, then as she shook her head, "It's official, the Arabs have bought us out, and guess what?"

"I can't guess, what is it?"

"Sir Humphrey is still the chairman. Apparently he was working with the Arabs all along".

"I'm not surprised", said Emily, "I always thought he was a devious character".

"Not here though", Bryant added, "This is going to be a separate part of the company, that reminds me, I've got to get Abdullah Karim to telephone London, I couldn't reach him at the hotel".

"He came with me in the car" said Emily, "I've left him in the lab with Peter and the Sheikh".

"Good", said Bryant, "I'll nip down and see him".

As he left Emily ruffled Andrew's hair.

"That just leaves up now love, doesn't it?"

He touched her hand, then gently squeezed it.

"Come on", said Emily quietly, "Let's go and

see what's happening".

Abdullah saw them as they descended the stairs and beckoned them to follow him outside.

"The Sheikh is leaving", he said, "And you Mister Craig…" he said no more for the Sheikh swept out of the building and settled himself on the back of the she-camel that Ben Acate had rode to the factory.

"Up" he commanded, and the animal rose shudderingly to it's feet.

The Sheikh gazed down at the small group that watched and said,

"Abdullah tells me that I must leave for the airfield immediately".

"I'll take you in the car", Emily offered.

"And these noble beasts?" the Sheikh asked, "can they go in the car also?" he answered his own question, "No and they cannot stay here, they too need to feel the hot sand of the desert beneath their feet", he smiled at Andrew.

"I am told my brother the Prince Achmed, who knows more of business that I, has acquired this place of yours, and it will be known as the Kohani Chemical Company. This is good that our name shall live in your country. Abdullah tells me that you are to be placed in command and this is also good and I wish you success, you and Miss Lang", he steadied the camel as it became restless, "did I not say that destiny rules the lives of all men".

Before Andrew could answer, the Sheikh called out something in Arabic, then in English.

"Farewell my friends, and you Ben Acate, mind you serve Mister Craig well".

Ben Acate, seeing Miss Allen peering from the laboratory window, made a low bow.

"It shall be as you desire, I willingly place myself here to do my master's bidding".

Eddy Gates, until now a silent spectator at the rear of the group, asked,

"Shall I fetch some rope to tie those camels together so he can lead them like?"

The Sheikh looked down, then taking a small phial from his robe, sprinkled a tiny drop of liquid on the hindquarters of his mount. The other camels immediately began to take an interest and , as the Sheikh kicked his beast into motion, they fell in behind, necks outstretched, and as they disappeared through the iron gates, Andrew could almost swear they were wearing expectant grins on their faces.

"That's that then", stated Andrew, then turned to Abdullah "What's this about me being in charge? In charge of what? With the Sheikh gone, and his potion, we've got nothing to make have we?"

Peter Winfield spoke up.

"He's left some, and we're going to make more when we need it", he proffered a small bottle, "Here, then as it shed a few drops on Andrew's sleeve, Oops the top's loose".

Emily gasped, but Andrew said,

"That's all right, it doesn't have much effect in the open air".

"Anyone for coffee?" asked Bryant, but as Abdullah, Peter and Eddy Gates nodded acceptance, Emily shook her head and whispered,

"Can we ..er," she sounded hesitant, "Your choice? Can we go there?"

"Certainly", Andrew led the way then stared at Emily as she locked the door behind them, "You're not...?"

He said no more as Emily moved slowly

towards him.

"Feel it", she whispered, "Can you smell it? Taste it?"

"Could he?" his lips tingled, his skin felt hot and even the hairs on his arm prickled as Emily's soft mouth fastened on his.

Andrew's head spun, he could feel a passion rising within that made him weak-kneed. Trembling, he feverishly sought for the proven protection from the Aroma, his inhaler, found it, then a Emily kissed him again, he sank unresistingly to the floor, pulling her with him, and , as she began to undo the buttons of his shirt, with one last despairing motion, he threw the metallic tube as far away as he could then gave himself willingly, wholeheartedly to the influence of the aroma, and the power of Emily's love.......

The End

Made in the USA
Columbia, SC
14 June 2017